The Whole Picture

The Whole Picture

A Novel

Donald McCullough

RESOURCE *Publications* · Eugene, Oregon

THE WHOLE PICTURE
A Novel

Resource Publications
An Imprint of Wipf and Stock Publishers
199 W. 8th Ave., Suite 3
Eugene, OR 97401

www.wipfandstock.com

PAPERBACK ISBN: 978-1-7252-5472-5
HARDCOVER ISBN: 978-1-7252-5473-2
EBOOK ISBN: 978-1-7252-5474-9

Manufactured in the U.S.A.   NOVEMBER 18, 2019

To the memory of
The Rev. John H. McCullough
1926–2013

The most serious error in exposure is giving too little exposure, because detail is thereby lost in shadow areas that cannot be recovered through any processing or subsequent manipulation. For most photographs, therefore, we make the initial placement based on *the darkest area of the subject where we want to preserve detail in the image.*

—ANSEL ADAMS, *THE NEGATIVE*

For now we see in a mirror, dimly, but then we shall see face to face. Now I know only in part; then I will know fully, even as I have been fully known.

—ST. PAUL, *1 CORINTHIANS 13:12*

Contents

Prologue

"**D**addy, who is she?"

The girl, four or five years old, didn't take her eyes off the picture. I had held the door of the gallery for them as she finished the last leaky inch of an ice cream cone and her father nudged her inside, and for some reason, curiosity I suppose, I had followed them through the exhibit. She was more interested in the squeak of her rubber soles on the parquet than the photographs, but her father stationed her for a few seconds in front of each one—a white steeple impaling dark sky, cracked kelp lying in ruined tangles, ghostly redwoods haunting thick fog, sinuous foam marking the advance of an exhausted wave—until at last we stood in front of The Photograph.

That's how I've always thought of it: The Photograph.

The curator had carefully considered its placement, hanging it alone on a freestanding wall at the end of the room.

A man on the other side of me pushed his glasses up and said, to no one in particular, "Thought the original'd be bigger."

The black-and-white print was behind glass, bordered by a five-inch white matte and simple black frame. Near its lower right corner, an identification card was affixed to the wall:

Logan Stanhope
Nude on the Beach
Gelatin silver print
11 x 14 inches

A few strands of errant hair wafted above the face that looked out from the picture. The left side reflected light that even in tones of gray seemed golden, and the right side, below the cheekbone, hid in dark shadow. With the exception of the eyes, the individual parts were unremarkable, perhaps flawed—nose too sharp, cheekbones too pronounced, mouth too large— but together, they were the alchemical formula to make common elements precious, transforming themselves into incandescent beauty.

Her breasts were visible, swelling into the lower half of the picture. On one, a small smudge of sand clung to damp skin, resembling a dash of cinnamon on whipped cream.

"Oh, oh," the girl said, putting her left hand over her mouth and giggling. "How come she's not dressed?"

Her father ignored the question.

"Daddy, who is she?" Receiving no answer, she raised her voice and pulled her father's arm with each word, "Who . . . *is* . . . she?"

"I don't know, sweetheart."

Then she turned and looked up at me. "Do you know who she is?"

One

Lunch with Owen Lambert never went past one o'clock. The founder of the firm didn't squander billable hours. So after the server left with their orders, he laid his glasses on the white tablecloth and announced the reason for their meeting.

"We had high expectations when we hired you in 1991. Yale Law Review, further study at Oxford, clerkship with O'Connor." During this litany he squeezed fingertips for enumeration. The skin around his knuckles sagged after seventy-two years but his fingernails were rounded and buffed. French cuffs, linked with black onyx, slid out from under navy pinstripe, and three points of a white handkerchief rose sharply from the suit's breast pocket. The knot of his tie had been perfectly constructed under a widespread collar. Not a white hair on head or eyebrows had strayed from its assigned place. "We have not been disappointed. You've earned revenue for the firm and respect from your colleagues." He paused to sip iced tea and to allow John Stanhope time to savor the compliment.

"Thank you," John said. "The firm's confidence means a great deal."

"Well, to the point. With Mark's retirement next year, we'll need a managing partner. Others have a vote, certainly, but I'm prepared to lend my influence to your candidacy."

John was one of the youngest partners—thirty-five—and seldom spoke in business meetings. The fantasy had occasionally slipped into his daydreams, but he wasn't sure, if it ever came down to it, he would want the job: it would mean less time for his own clients and more stress in organizing one hundred sixty-three partners in L.A., Seattle, and Denver.

On the other hand, managing partner.

"Mr. Lambert, I'm honored. Not sure what else to say, except I'll consider it carefully."

"I hope you will."

And that was that. The end of formal business punctured the tire of their conversation, and it bounced and thudded through prawn salads toward the exit ramp with small talk—how are the grandchildren? any vacation plans for summer? what about the Dodgers?

Nothing more was said about the offer until the elevator door in the Arco Towers opened and they entered a reception area with burnished gold letters on a mahogany wall that declared *Lambert and Wilson, Attorneys-at-Law*.

"Thank you for lunch," John said, "and for your confidence."

"I believe it's well placed."

They shook hands and walked down opposite hallways.

John's assistant, Bernice, was on the telephone. She held up a forefinger, sign language that meant, *Wait, I'm almost finished*. An African-American of ample proportions, physically and in other ways, she had convinced John that if the world were a fairer place, he would be working for her and thankful for the opportunity. She had learned how to care for others as the eldest of eight children born to a Louisiana shrimp fisherman. She knew people, Bernice Carter did, and though she used that knowledge on John, she also used it for him.

"Yes, Mrs. Schmidt," she said, "you know how eager Mr. Stanhope will be to help you. He'll call this afternoon."

John shook his head and contorted his face into exaggerated misery. She pretended not to notice and assured Mrs. Schmidt of his dedication before setting down the receiver.

"Sorry, John, but Schmidt happens."

"And thanks to you, I'm up to my neck in it. Makes me want to double my fees."

"So, you doing it?"

"Doubling my fees?"

"You know what I mean." She arched her left eyebrow.

"You're spooky."

"You don't have to be Sherlock Holmes for this one. Mark Anderson's retirement around the corner, lunch with The Man, and besides, what choice does he have given his sorry options?"

"I suppose that's a compliment."

4

"Here's today's mail." She slid it across the desk, her fingers lingering on the top envelope. "I've gone through everything. Except this. Might be something you should open."

The return address said "Marshall Folger, Attorney-at-Law, 500 Franklin Street, Fort Bragg, California 95437."

John made no comment about the envelope but took it to his office and placed it on the corner of his desk. He scanned his emails and thumbed through the recent issue of *ABA Journal*; he tackled a pile of procrastination that had been gaining altitude for days, dictating letters, initialing contracts, signing vouchers, and writing a check to the UCLA Alumni Fund; he cleaned the drawer in front of him because a man who can't keep order in his desk has no business managing a law firm, and delinquent paper clips and desiccated rubber bands and faded expense receipts were undermining the case for his promotion; and he *almost* called Mrs. Schmidt.

Anything but open the envelope from Fort Bragg.

Bernice saw it when she set a stack of documents on his desk to sign. She immediately looked outside, and the deliberate disregard of her bulging bloodshot eyes felt like a rebuke.

"I'll open it when I'm ready."

"Did I say anything?"

Alone again, he stared at nothing in particular, except maybe ghosts rising from his memory. He wanted nothing to do with them, and because the envelope had summoned them, he wanted nothing to do with it. But it would not leave him alone.

Eventually he surrendered. Inside was a letter and, enclosed in celluloid sleeves, four negatives, each four inches by five inches. He lifted them to the light. One was too familiar, the others a mystery.

July 2, 2001

Mr. John Stanhope
Lambert and Wilson
555 S. Flower Street
Los Angeles, California 90071

Dear Mr. Stanhope:

I regret to inform you that your father, Logan Stanhope, passed away on June 11, 2001. The cause of death was cancer, malignant melanoma.

The trustee of your father's estate has asked me to send you the enclosed negatives.

I must also say that, pursuant to my client's instructions, I may not divulge further information concerning your father's death or the disposition of his remaining property.

My condolences,
Marshall Folger

Still holding the letter and negatives, John walked to the window. Smog diffused the sun's light and dimmed the city's lines. He stood there, motionless, until a gathering weight pushed him to the floor. With no energy to rise, he leaned back against the window and extended his legs.

His father.

John had not spoken to him since he was sixteen, with the exception of two awkward calls when he graduated from high school and college.

Now he was dead.

And he left nothing but four negatives. One was *Nude on the Beach*.

Bernice knocked and didn't wait for an answer before entering. She paused briefly and then walked across the room and slowly, not easily, sat herself down beside him. Neither spoke for what might have been a long time.

John said, "It's my father."

"Thought so. The only time you mentioned him, you said he might be in Mendocino. Fort Bragg's close, isn't it?"

"The letter said he died."

The silence between them grew until it seemed necessary, until it became a messenger of mercy, until it vanished with the ringing of the telephone. Bernice ignored the intrusion, stayed put, and John received her bulky matter-of-factness as a gift: tired perfume and stale coffee, labored breathing and gurgling stomach, dimpled knees and diminutive feet—the body's concreteness bestowed an uncomplicated comfort. John had to squint to discern the designs on her toenails.

"I haven't talked with him for a long time. We've had a . . . it's been difficult."

"What's that?" she asked, pointing to the negatives on the other side of him.

"My inheritance."

She covered his hand with hers. It was warm and slightly damp. For a few seconds he imagined how good it would feel if she would cover him with her whole body, if she would smother him and hold him in place and keep him from following memories that wanted to take him down dangerous roads.

"Listen, John, you're not going to get anything done this afternoon—anything, that is, that I won't have to clean up later. It'll be easier for both of us if you get out of here."

"What about Mrs. Schmidt?"

"Leave her to me." She hauled herself up and straightened her dress.

"Bernice?" He waited for her to look down at him. "Thanks."

"I'm better at typing depositions."

Twenty minutes later he walked through her office and waved goodbye.

"Just remember," she said, pointing at the center of her chest, "the father stays right here. Can't get rid of him."

Who was the father in him? The void between them had had enough oxygen to sustain bitterness and anger, but his death now emptied the emptiness, creating a vacuum that sucked into it colliding images and long-suppressed feelings, and John sensed he would have to ask again a question he had already answered and kept frozen in hard certainties, a question that maybe he had not dared to reconsider because he lacked the courage: Who was his father, really? Who was this man who, for the moment, pressed upon his thoughts with more immediacy than traffic in the northbound lanes of the Pasadena Freeway?

Two

After a few miles of maneuvering between trucks and steroidal SUVs, questions about his father were improbably edged out by the knot of Owen Lambert's tie.

How did he do it?

John asked himself that question every morning as he tried to replicate the elongated symmetrical four-in-hand, and he was asking it again, wondering if maybe the tie was actually a half-Windsor and if the quality of its material had anything to do with it, if perhaps he should lay down large bucks for a Hermès, say, or a Talbot.

He was a child reaching for his security blanket. To protect himself from terrors of the night, John wrapped himself in well-ordered perfectionism. It wasn't a conscious strategy. You don't one day decide an impeccable knot will protect you from monsters under your bed, or those beneath your consciousness, for that would mean acknowledging them in the first place, the very thing you want to avoid. Instead, you gradually accumulate habits, moving from polishing shoes to repairing every ding on your car to signing papers on a new townhouse three blocks south of Colorado Boulevard that has white walls and black granite countertops and stainless steel appliances, and feels virginal, unburdened by a past, an immaculate blank space, like a starched collar waiting for the life you're trying to get perfectly tied.

To that townhouse he now headed as Friday afternoon's traffic drained onto Arroyo Parkway and inched toward the San Gabriels. Two years earlier, when the realtor showed it to him, the mountains were concealed in clouds, as they were a month later when he moved in. But during his first night as owner an entire range erupted. Every morning after that, except in rain, he drank coffee on the balcony, and gratitude, like the range itself, rose up from deep inside him. To whom it should be rendered, he was no longer sure. He was sure, however, that big pieces of his life—job, home, routines—had settled into place. Not everything, true. A wife and children were still missing, but feelings of incompleteness, he told himself, were senseless. Families can deliver as much pain as pleasure.

And now, proof in point, the family of his birth was messing with him, disrupting his tidy world. Memories were like smoke wafting around him that had to be funneled down, tornado-like, into the compartments where they belonged. His father, especially now that he was dead, could not distract from the prospect of becoming the managing partner of Lambert and Wilson.

John went upstairs to change into his swimsuit and get *The Brothers Karamazov*. His reading plan was a rotation of genres: self-improvement, biography, and literature. Dostoevsky was on everyone's list of great authors, but he had been struggling. Talk about family pain! And the proliferation of names! Alexei, Alyosha, Alyoshenka, Lyosha, and more—for the same character? But he was a hundred pages into it, committed for the long haul.

He walked through the breezeway to the backside of the building. The pool was large, bordered on all sides by wide swaths of grass cut as short as a putting green. Only two residents ever used it—John and Joe Carmenetti. Joe was a bookie on the wrong side of the law, almost certainly in the employ of an organization. His office was a lounge chair with a table next to it holding a bottle of water, two cellphones, the daily racing form, a pen, and several sheets of water-dissolving paper from China. Two legs of the table were always an inch from the pool. When police ran across the courtyard, which John witnessed from his balcony one unforgettable evening, Joe flicked his notes into eight feet of water and chlorine, leaving not a single soggy scrap of evidence.

John thought maybe Joe trusted him because he assumed lawyerly confidentiality, or maybe because John once took Joe's fourteen-year-old son visiting from New Jersey to a Dodgers game, or maybe because loneliness had gotten the better of good judgment. Regardless, John had learned far more than he had wanted to know.

"Hey, Perry Mason," Joe said. "What's up?" Joe was at work, dressed in his customary white t-shirt and baggy blue shorts. "What're you doing home?"

"Keeping an eye on you."

John arranged himself on the opposite side of the pool, wanting to signal a lack of interest in Joe's latest "opportunity," which would likely involve a fixed race at Santa Anita.

"Hot date tonight?" Joe had made it his responsibility to monitor John's romantic life.

During the past six months John and Megan O'Connell had settled into a pattern. Fridays they had dinner at a restaurant, often went to a movie or concert, and usually ended up at his place for the rest of the weekend. Saturday morning they went for a long run and ate a leisurely breakfast, followed by an afternoon of shopping for groceries and other chores, with the evening devoted to cooking in his kitchen, taking turns as Executive Chef, the competitiveness drawing upon ever more exotic recipes, culminating in John's triumphal Moroccan Lamb Tagine with Pine Nut Couscous. Sundays they went to All Saints Episcopal Church to sing in the choir.

That's where they met: Megan (alto) sat directly in front of John (tenor), and after a few weeks of smiles and eye contact, they began talking after practice, and then visiting until the custodian wanted to turn off the lights, and then moving across the street to a wine bar. She had short red hair, sometimes spiked at odd angles, a faint dusting of freckles across her nose, and unnerving green eyes that gave the impression they saw more than you wanted to reveal.

Neither had uttered the m-word, but when it came up in movies, say, or in conversation with others, a slight tension arose between them. John was afraid that if he gave even the smallest opening, she would slip through with the agility of a running back. At the very least, Megan argued, she wanted to move in with him. She missed him during the week and was tired of carrying things back and forth. For reasons he didn't really understand, he was always relieved to have her return to her own apartment on Sunday.

But it was still Friday as he sat by the pool, and he looked forward to telling Megan about his conversation with Owen Lambert, though it would likely intensify her push toward marriage. It wasn't easy concentrating on Dostoyevsky. His mind wandered toward seeing himself as the one to whom colleagues went with problems, the one responsible for keeping the firm working smoothly and making money, and the further he strayed from Russia, the more he realized how much he wanted the job, how much he had always wanted it, and he couldn't wait to talk about the possibility. That evening, right after wine was poured, he would offer a toast to . . . what? He'd have to come up with something creative.

It was time to quit the pool. John thought he could slip away with just a wave, but before he got halfway down the breezeway, he heard Joe say loudly enough for everyone in the neighborhood, "Don't forget, kid, you need advice about women, I'm available. Reasonable rates, too, cheaper than lawyers."

"I'll keep that in mind."

"Will Megan be here tomorrow?"

"Probably."

"Highlight of my week! If you had any sense, you'd get her to a priest, pronto."

Three

The Purple Gecko's hardwood floors, live music, and tight tables made noise that shouted, What a crowd! What fun! Trolling singles loved it, as well as couples bored with conversation. John and Megan wouldn't have given it a second chance had it not been for the outdoor seating. Passing cars and trucks and motorcycles seemed hushed compared with the indoor traffic. They were given a table near the patio's perimeter, where a cool mist descended from pipes hidden amidst hanging baskets of fuchsias.

A server soon appeared who introduced himself as Fernando. John and Megan both chose the special, grilled halibut with mango salsa, and to accompany it, a Sauvignon Blanc from New Zealand.

Fernando returned with their bottle and threw himself into The Presentation of Wine as if he were a theater student at Pasadena City College. He fussed with the ice bucket, setting its stand in its proper place, and then, pausing for complete attention, twisted the screw into the cork and popped it free with movements employing most of his upper body. He offered the cork for examination and poured a swallow for tasting, and John played his part by swirling and sniffing and sipping.

John was more than ready when they lifted their goblets toward each other. It had been difficult for him to contain the dam-bursting force of his news as he opened the door of her geriatric Honda and waited for her to unfasten the seatbelt and check the status of her lipstick in the rearview mirror. Now was the moment.

But she said, "I have a toast. To dreams coming true."

Had she heard? Had Bernice spilled the beans? He imagined the unlikely before the obvious. It took a few seconds to realize she had her own news.

"I was given a show!" she said. "Not a big one, just a relatively un-known artist. But if it goes well, more will follow." She cocked her head, the way she did after an advantageous move on a board game.

Megan had graduated from the University of Southern California in Art History, and earlier in the summer had received an M.B.A. from the same school. She wanted to direct a museum someday. So when the Norton Simon offered an internship, she jumped at the opportunity, and when a year later they offered a position as administrative assistant, she didn't exactly jump but took it anyway, hoping it would lead to something better. She was eventually promoted to assistant curator, which, as far as John could tell, was still largely grunt work but a sign of their growing confidence in her.

"Congratulations, that's great." John asked questions about the artist and, while she was answering, debated with himself about what to say next. He didn't want to detract from her news.

"What's the matter?" she asked. "You seem sort of subdued."

"I'm happy. Really happy."

"But what?" Her skeptical eyes weren't going to let go until they squeezed the truth out of him.

"It's just that I have news too, and honestly I don't want to play I Can Top That.

"Let it rip, buddy. We can take two good things in one day."

"OK, then." John smiled and lifted his goblet again. "To the wisdom—the amazing perception—of Owen Lambert." They clinked, and he sloshed around a mouthful of wine like a reviewer for *The Wine Spectator*, and slowly, with flair to rival Fernando's, set down his goblet.

She crinkled her forehead, baffled. "You want to explain?"

He wasn't going to toss out a punchline with no preparation. He described The California Club, its reek of wealth and power, what they had had to eat, on and on, everything he could remember. He was pumping the drama, increasing the anticipation, but he noticed the warning coming from slightly raised eyebrows across from him.

"Yeah, yeah," she muttered, in a this-had-better-be-good tone.

When he finally said the words "managing partner," she yelped and reached out to grab him. But the flight path of her hand hadn't taken into account the location of a nearly-full goblet. Glass shattered and wine flowed toward John's lap.

"Oh no," she said, putting a hand over her mouth. She built a dam with her napkin, but the river simply altered course. So she waved it away as inconsequential and jumped out of her chair and fell on John with a hug.

"John, that's fabulous, I'm so proud of you!"

"We're causing a scene."

"Who cares? Get up."

He had no choice.

The lip lock won scattered applause from around the patio. Three women at a nearby table signaled thumbs up and winked. Fernando arrived with a salad in each hand and said, "What have we here, a little celebration?" But his smile faded when he saw the table. John and Megan apologized and helped clear space for the salads, and Fernando, when his hands were free, picked up shards of broken glass.

Not until John bent over to retrieve his napkin did he see Sauvignon Blanc on his pants in an undesirable location. He felt as exposed as Adam after sampling forbidden fruit and tried to turn the napkin into a loincloth, sitting down quickly—too quickly to notice that during the hugging and kissing the wine had continued to flow onto his chair, thereby wetting his pants in the other undesirable location.

Megan said, "So, any more toasts?"

That started them laughing. And when John reported that his backside was also wet, they went over an edge, like children in school or church, laughing at their laughing.

"Stop it!" John whispered. He looked away, holding his breath.

"Right," Megan said, nodding gravely. She took a deep breath. "Well," she said, prim and proper, "isn't this salad nice? Is this fennel, do you think?"

Just when John thought it might be safe to make eye contact, she said, "If Fernando doesn't bring me another glass soon, I'll have to suck your pants." This caused a new explosion, and now she surrendered to a power beyond her control, putting her elbows on the table and covering her face with her hands.

"Seriously Megan, they're going to send bouncers over here."

Adding to the commotion, his cellphone played "Amazing Grace," the ring Bernice had programmed for herself. He would have ignored it, but Bernice rarely called after hours.

"Sorry to bother you, John." Her tone was full of concern.

"It's fine, go ahead."

"Half-an-hour ago, as I was leaving, Clarisse—remember her? runs the copy room?—she ran into me and said something like, 'Way to spice up an afternoon, girl!' Apparently someone stopped by my office around two this afternoon." She paused for the implication sink in. "When we were on the floor."

"Shit." The word was out before John could check himself.

Megan put down her salad fork.

"Rumor has it . . . well, you can imagine."

"That's crazy! We'd have shut the door if we were doing it! How many people know?"

Megan's smile vanished.

"No idea. Clarisse heard it from two or three. Sorry to drop this on you. I thought you'd want to know. Before Monday."

"Thanks, I guess. See you then."

Megan's eyes went to work on John.

"It's not as bad as it sounds," he said.

"It couldn't be."

Fernando approached with the halibut as if entering a radioactive zone. He jauntily asked, "Do we need more time with our salads?" Not waiting for an answer, he set the halibut in front of them, refreshed their wine, and escaped.

John looked across the patio a few moments, and then quietly spoke. "This afternoon I received word my father died. I didn't mention it earlier because he hasn't been part of my life for years." Hearing himself, he felt like an ass, a first-class ass, the archetypal form of pure asshood. What sort of son would laugh uncontrollably the day he heard his father died?

For some reason he said nothing about the four negatives.

Confusion settled in Megan's eyes. She began a few sentences without ever finishing one, as if too many were jostling inside her for any to surface intact.

"You don't need to worry about Bernice," he said. "Nothing's going on."

"It's not Bernice I'm worried about, John. It's *you*. What the hell is it with you, anyway? I mean, you tell me great news—managing partner, no less—and then confess to rolling around on the floor—"

"No, we weren't rolling around—"

15

"I'm not finished, in case you hadn't noticed." The color in her face had risen. "Whatever you were doing, you start a rumor that could sink your career, and 'Oh, by the way, my father died.' Your *father*, for God's sake!"

The conversation slid into silence as they picked through their food.

Fernando had their check at the ready, undoubtedly relieved to hear they had no interest in dessert or coffee.

John scribbled a hefty tip on the credit card bill as atonement.

"We ready?" he asked.

She nodded silently.

On the way to Megan's car, John attempted to hold her hand, but she kept it busy doing something in her purse, maybe looking for keys.

"Listen, John, you need to be alone tonight."

"No, please, I want you with me."

He did not know what to expect until he turned down his street and saw Megan's headlights behind him.

Four

" **Y**our father. A photographer, right? That's about all I know."
No escaping it now: he had to focus on his father, and in an instant, John was no longer with Megan but in San Diego, and he saw the
original, the clearer rendition, of what was in the mirror every morning—
blond hair with cowlick at the hairline, blue eyes with lupine intensity, and
a broad smile with high-voltage charm. He saw chinos stained with darkroom chemicals and yellowed fingers packing a pipe from a red Amphora
tin, and he felt stubble scraping his cheek and breath warming his ear ("just
between us guys"), and he heard arguments about going to church. John
was back in a place where memories like a sharp knife sliced through scar
tissue: he saw his mother sitting at the kitchen table, a letter in front of her,
fingers raking through disheveled hair, and he heard her say, "He's leaving
us, not coming home."

"You still here?" Megan asked.

"Not really."

He described, as best he could, what he had been thinking, and each
memory jostled loose others, and the suppressed feelings of the day ani-
mated the monologue, filling it with irrelevant details, and it occurred to
him that he was making it sound like a Norman Rockwell painting.

"But things changed. We had a normal life, I guess, until I was sixteen,
or as normal as you can have with a mother whose emotions were a roller
coaster we all had to ride. Then Dad left us. Me as much as Mom. Left me
to cope with her moods, to lift her up or bring her down, depending. It
wasn't easy."

"Why did he leave?"

"Another woman. He went his way, we went ours. Hearing about his death this afternoon—it disturbed the status quo, that's all. End of story."

"I doubt it." Megan put her arm around John and drew him closer. "I have other questions. Plenty of them. But I won't push you, not tonight. We'll take it in small doses. Maybe another teaspoon tomorrow, and another the next day. OK?"

What more did she want to know? What more did she *need* to know? Her curiosity was understandable, but could the past be excavated from the sediment of confusion and misunderstanding that surrounded it when it was still the present? Could hardened layers of misperception be chiseled off to uncover a clean artifact? And supposing this could happen, could the current confusion and misunderstanding be set aside to make an objective evaluation? Could anyone ever really know another person?

John did not express these questions but nodded his assent to another teaspoon tomorrow and possibly the next day, happy his commitment extended only two days.

Megan kissed his cheek. An offering of peace, or maybe an invitation? She stood up, took him by the hand, and led him into the bedroom. She undressed on the way to the bed, and John collected her strewn clothes and laid them on a chair.

"Would you hurry up?" she said. "You're as fussy as an old lady!"

They pressed against each other as if they couldn't get close enough. Their hands followed every impulse, touching, caressing, wanting to be everywhere at once. But when he cupped her breasts, a picture appeared unbidden and unwanted. He tried to shut it out, to stay with Megan, but the picture persisted, took him to another time and place. He was still aroused, and that sickened him because now the arousal felt connected to shame and pain and anger. Self-disgust flooded over him like ice water and his desire shriveled.

Megan pulled away. "What's the matter?"

John rolled over on his back, unable to speak. How could he tell her that when he touched her breasts, he saw others—those of a woman on a beach, those in a photograph that had haunted his youth, those that had weirdly linked his sexuality with his father, his desire with his anger, and which for years became anger at his desire? It was too much to explain. So he said nothing.

She waited, patiently at first and then, it seemed, with increasing ir-
ritation. He knew it wasn't his inability to perform that upset her; it was his
impotence of speech, his flaccid tongue.

Fifteen or twenty minutes of silence became a wall.

Megan got out of bed, walked into faint light leaking through the window, searched through her clothes, and stepped into panties.

"Where the hell did you put my bra?"

"Megan—"

"John, I know you've had a long day." Her words were restrained, quiet.
"But making love is about more than you getting inside me. It's also about
me getting inside you. Not that that has ever happened. A virgin, that's what
you are. I care for you, John, but I should not have to drag everything out
of you."

She walked out of the room and down the stairs. John did not hear the
front door slam because by then he had buried his head in the pillow and
was sobbing.

Before long he was batting in a game with Owen Lambert pitching,
and after striking out, he went to the dugout where Megan was sitting and
she pushed him to the ground and crawled on top of him and he could
see over her shoulder other people, people from his office, but he didn't
care because her body was a heating pad for strained muscles and Bernice
whispered that this would create rumors. That's when he woke.

It was two-fifteen.

Five

The next morning John lingered on the balcony, drinking a third cup of coffee and doing *The New York Times* crossword puzzle. All but six words, not bad for a Saturday. The cool, clean air sharpened every rock on the mountains like a German lens.

Hope, if not dancing in him, was at least limping, thanks to a large dose of caffeine that countered the depressive effects of Bernice's call and Megan's departure. He had buzzed himself into the conviction that rumors could be dispelled on Monday, if they hadn't already blown over, and that Megan's temper, never to be underestimated, would subside once she saw his willingness to let her inside, as she put it.

Through the rest of the day John attempted to ignore the cryptic negatives, not wanting to grant his father power over him, especially not from the grave. But it's a law that the harder you try not to think about purple lizards, say, a herd of them will haunt your days and trouble your nights. So he kept holding up the negatives to incandescent light and then to sunlight, as if that might make a difference, and he tried to imagine the clear places black and the black places white. One was indecipherable, largely a dark blankness. Another seemed to be a building. The third, he guessed, was of trees. And the fourth—well, there she was.

It was too late and thus too hot for a run, so John spent a couple of hours working on *The Brothers Karamazov* and swimming laps.

"Where's the gorgeous one?" Joe asked. "Wriggling into a bikini, I hope."

He was freshly shaven, as always on Saturday, and his t-shirt had the brightness and creases of one fresh from its package. But the spiffiness was undermined by the shirt's slide on his paunch, revealing patches of flesh beneath a shag carpet.

"Sorry, not here."

Joe wanted an explanation. Where was she, anyway? Was there a problem between them? Is she finally ready for a more mature man? He renewed his offer of counseling.

"You know what?" John said. "It's none of your business."

That afternoon John sat at the keyboard of his Kawai, glassy as a Marine's shoes, standing at attention against the white wall, and he practiced sections of *The Well-Tempered Clavier*. He had started piano lessons in the third grade, going once a week to Mrs. Kravis, with her merciless metronome and box of gold stars. His mother had imagined the day he would play gospel songs at Holy Spirit Chapel, which he soon did, banging out "Power in the Blood" and "I Love to Tell the Story" like Jimmy Swaggart, or so he imagined, but his skills and tastes eventually expanded to a life-saving discovery, Johann Sebastian Bach, who supplied structure amidst the turmoil of his home, a balanced world of point and counterpoint, a channel for unpredictable emotions. Later he would say that a good fugue can be worth hours of psychotherapy. So he continued studying piano at UCLA, first as an elective and then as a major. Fellow students praised his technical mastery—the word "wizardry" had been heard—and this nurtured dreams of becoming a concert pianist, but his advisor's formal evaluation following a recital in his junior year dashed them. The professor affirmed John's skill but said that "something" was missing, that he "heard notes but missed the music," and he used an analogy, perhaps offhandedly, that had life-altering consequences: everything had been rendered with legalistic precision, but more like a judge applying law than an artist creating beauty.

John had been wounded, but even at the time knew it was a gracious wounding. He never let go of his love of music, and this was what drew him to All Saints. He attended a concert of Bach's *St. Matthew Passion*, and the excellence drew him back for the 11:00 Eucharist, after which, as a postlude, the organist played "Toccata and Fugue in D Minor," pushing the volume pedal so the improbable bass notes shook the sanctuary's foundation. What would happen the following Sunday? John kept wondering, week after week, and thus he landed in the church of his grandfather, an Episcopal bishop in New England.

John's father left the faith of his family and never entered a sanctuary except to photograph a wedding or under marital duress at Christmas and Easter. But his mother stayed true to her own upbringing—her mother had dedicated herself to carrying on the work of Aimee Semple MacPherson—and kept them in the front pew of a real church. She considered the Episcopal Church near kin to the Whore of Babylon, with its "smells and bells and book-prayers," a dangerous place to be in the event of the Rapture. They attended a chapel where John went forward to accept Jesus and get filled with the Spirit more times than he could count until he finally gave up. If he was going to get saved, God would have to take care of it himself. Exhaustion, more than anything, had turned him away from the church, but music had brought him back. In the Anglican liturgy he found a way to recenter himself week after week. As he stood and kneeled, sang and prayed, listened and confessed, his own beliefs didn't seem to matter much as the centuries-old tradition anchored him to a place that felt both ordered and good.

That's not to say his thoughts didn't wander around like a curious puppy, especially that weekend without Megan. The summer choir was on duty, so he sat with the congregation in the protean colors of stained-glass. The girl in front of him wore jeans so low that her kneeling was hard to ignore as he confessed that he had followed too much the devices and desires of his own heart, even as that heart hauled him off to other times and places. Was he the only one with this problem? Were others wholly concentrated on the business at hand? Or was the girl in front of him remembering what she had done the evening before in her boyfriend's car? And was the guy next to him catching the eye of someone in the choir, maybe another guy? And was his wife angry at him for ignoring her all weekend? And was the priest, for that matter, having his own problems, maybe worried about the sermon he wrote under the inspiration of inebriation and which he would soon be delivering while hungover? Were we secret sensualists, all of us, joining forces for an hour on Sunday to cut a clearing in the thicket of our desires for the possibility that a ray or two of transcendence might descend?

Besides wondering these things, John scanned the worshippers for Megan and, especially during the sermon, rehearsed his side of the impending conversation. He would persuade her to come home with him, he would show her the negatives, he would somehow prove his vulnerability. But he didn't see her, not even when everyone filed forward for the Eucharist.

Should he call or wait for her to make the first move? By the time he got home, he couldn't wait any longer. But she did not answer her cellphone. About ten minutes later, however, his rang.

"I was playing with my niece," she began, cool as a polar cap.

"You're in Santa Barbara?"

"Yes, Molly's been begging me to come up." Molly was Megan's older sister, the wife of an orthodontist and mother of three kids with perfectly straight teeth. Megan was the fourth of six children born to a detective in the Santa Barbara Police Department and his tiny, endlessly talkative wife. The members of her family were close, always looking for excuses to get together. She had already dragged him to three birthday parties and an anniversary celebration and was no doubt assuming they would go up for Thanksgiving and Christmas.

"Uh," he said. "I didn't mean to hurt your feelings." He paused for her to say it was all right or she understood, but she waited for him to continue. "Something else happened I didn't mention."

"Oh really? What a surprise."

"My father bequeathed me something through his attorney. I want to show it to you."

"What is it?"

"It's too hard to explain on the phone. When can I see you?"

"We had plenty of time Friday evening, didn't we? But did you show it to me then? Of course not. And why is that, John?"

"Well—"

"Let me answer for you. It's because you have to be backed into a corner with no other option before revealing anything about yourself—unless it fits *your* needs, fits *your* schedule, fits *your* everything-in-its place tightass world."

"Megan, I'm sorry."

"I'm sorry, this relationship is no longer fitting *my* needs, and I have no idea when seeing whatever it is you want to show me will fit into *my* schedule."

That's how she ended the conversation.

Six

John didn't sleep much Sunday night, flinging his body around the bed in search of cool sheets. But the sun lightened his darkness and coffee got him to the Rose Bowl and Brookside Park.

The trail was crowded with runners, walkers, and bicyclists. As he merged into sweating traffic he planned his day: he would follow up on whatever Mrs. Schmidt wanted, study the contract between City of Angels Waste Management and Myerson Construction, finish researching a bill before the state Assembly that would modify the code on contracts, he would not accept Megan's outburst as a farewell but would eat massive portions of humble pie and demonstrate willingness—no, *eagerness*—to change, and finally, he would make an appointment with Owen Lambert to tell him that yes he would definitely like to be the managing partner. Endorphins were doing their happy work, injecting cask-strength 100-proof optimism into his bloodstream, and he knew, without doubt, that he was going to have a good day, that he was a man with a future, that he wasn't someone to be taken lightly, that he wouldn't take crap from anyone—no rumors from cheap voyeurs, no petulance from an emotional girlfriend, and certainly no nonsense from a dead father.

By the time he was driving to the office and his system had reached homeostasis, he knew that he was going to do whatever Bernice told him to do.

Bernice would have had a difficult weekend, worrying less about herself than what rumors could do to John. So on his way from the parking garage, he stopped at the Plaza and bought a dozen roses at Iris's Flower Shop and, better yet, an apple fritter at Starbucks, which according to Bernice contained all essential food groups for a perfectly balanced meal.

"Oh my, you dear man, I'd wrap my fat arms around you if we weren't in enough trouble already."

"I could shut the door."

"Which is what we should have done on Friday."

"You really think this'll have legs?"

"Enough for a marathon."

"Nah, we should put it to rest pretty quickly."

"That so? Have you figured out what to say we were doing on the floor? With your head on my shoulder."

"My head was on your shoulder?"

"And your hand on my thigh."

"No, you're exaggerating."

"You were upset."

"I'm sorry, Bernice."

"Don't apologize. Most fun I've had in a long time. But we'll need an explanation. Half a dozen questions will hit me between here and the restroom."

What should they say? That she was comforting him? Why? He hated bringing his father into it but saw no alternative. The death of a parent engenders sympathy.

"Let's just say my father died but I don't want to talk about it. That has the advantage of being the truth."

"That's living on the edge, for a lawyer."

"No need to be a smart-mouth after I brought you an apple fritter."

Her "To Do" list wasn't much different from his, except it had more of Mrs. Schmidt than he wanted on a Monday. Leona Schmidt, as Bernice put it, pushed his buttons. He was not alone. The mere mention of her name could drain color from the faces of the other partners. One of them said, "An hour with that woman and I need an appointment with Sigmund Friggin' Freud."

Midway through the morning Bernice beeped him on the intercom. "John, that meeting you wanted with Mr. Lambert? He can see you at three this afternoon."

"Perfect, thanks."

As he walked past her desk on the way to the appointment he said, "Here goes." She didn't respond. Her head was partially hidden behind roses, and she didn't look up. "You OK?"

"Fine."

"What's the matter?"

"I told you, I'm fine. Just go or you'll be late."

Owen Lambert's assistant, Ruth Corrigan, had been with him a long time. No one knew how long, but she gave the impression it had been before the adoption of the Magna Carta. Her white hair had been sprayed into unconditional surrender and absolute obedience. There had been speculation about whether she ever removed the pearls from around her neck.

"Good afternoon, Mr. Stanhope. Mr. Lambert is ready for you." Her smile, pure distillate of professional sincerity, meant you never knew where you stood with her.

Mr. Lambert's office had floor-to-ceiling windows for two walls, with Lady Justice on a pedestal in the corner between them. Books (federal and state law) covered the third wall, and diplomas, citations, and photographs of politicians hung on the fourth. Ronald Reagan, Pete Wilson, and George W. Bush draped arms around Mr. Lambert and flashed smiles that expressed gratitude for big contributions. The oriental rug, John estimated, was worth more than his townhouse. A massive desk sat in front of the Republicans, and on it were photographs of what must have been his wife, children, and grandchildren.

Mr. Lambert motioned for John to sit in one of the chairs facing his desk.

"Hello, John. Glad we could meet today. Coffee?"

"No, thanks."

"You're here, I assume, to follow up on Friday's conversation."

"Yes, sir. I'm deeply committed to the firm, as you know, and want to serve it to the best of my ability. If you believe this means moving into management, I'd be delighted to accept your support."

Mr. Lambert said nothing. He did not smile. Not one muscle in his body moved, until he stood and walked to the window.

John felt his pulse accelerate.

Without turning toward John, Mr. Lambert said, "I appreciate your loyalty to the firm. I trust I've made clear how grateful we are for your work." Then he faced John. "However, I've had to reconsider my offer."

John was paralyzed, unable to breathe.

"Part of the responsibility of our managing partner is to set an example, to help maintain the firm's image. You understand what I'm saying?"

John felt as if every book in the office had fallen on his chest. He had to force himself to take in air to get out a response. "Yes, of course, I've always tried to—"

"To be blunt, John, your private life is none of my business. But a relationship with your assistant is dangerous these days. Surely you know this. Especially after the harassment cases we've handled. This would be troubling in itself, but then, taking the liberties you did on Friday afternoon, in full view of anyone who walked by—I'm surprised. And disappointed. That's not how I'd expect a managing partner to comport himself."

"Sir, I assure you, what happened Friday isn't what you imagine." As John spoke, Mr. Lambert walked back to his desk, sat on a corner of it, and folded his arms. "It's true we were on the floor. That was unwise, I know. But I wasn't myself. I had fallen in a kind of shock, I guess, and Bernice was comforting me. I had just received word my father passed away."

Mr. Lambert unfolded his arms and sat in the chair next to him. "I'm sorry, John. Was his death unexpected?"

Ambushed first by condemnation and then by concern, John's defenses fell and he started talking about his father, about how their relationship had been difficult and they hadn't spoken in nearly twenty years. He rambled on, probably incoherently, and at one point he wondered what Megan would think of him opening up to someone he barely knew.

In the soliloquy he must have mentioned the negatives because Mr. Lambert asked, "What do you think he was trying to tell you?"

"I have no idea. Frankly, I don't care." Mr. Lambert's slightly raised eyebrows encouraged John to reconsider. "Or I don't want to care."

Mr. Lambert turned toward pictures on the desk. His eyes seemed focused on something only he could see. His hand moved slowly, heavy with hesitation, to one near him. He grasped its gold frame and lifted it from the assembled collection. He studied it carefully, saying nothing except whatever he was saying to himself.

"Families," he said, as if the word carried a trainload of meaning and the mere utterance of it was a bond of understanding between them. "How about we take a break from considering your role in the firm? No need to rush a decision. Take time to process your loss, and then we'll come at it fresh."

"Thank you," John said, not realizing how much time it would take and what processing his loss would eventually involve.

Seven

How do you go from wallowing in the psychological muck of a dead father to untangling the legal complications of Mrs. Schmidt's estate? You keep things in boxes; you concentrate on *this* and then *that*, first one thing and then another. Life is a series of problems, and the way to survive is to keep them discrete. So with his father pursuing, Megan leaving, and his future wobbling, John got through the week by throwing himself into every case with the dedication of a championship boxer; he punched and counterpunched and danced around the ring with complete concentration, evaluating the complications and ramifications of every legal issue. And at home he followed the same strategy: he busied himself with hanging a painting Megan had given him for his birthday, he memorized Goldberg Variation #16 to play in a pathetic imitation of Glenn Gould, he washed hardwood floors, and he pretended to read *The Brothers Karamazov* as he constructed a case against Megan's insensitivity.

He ignored the negatives.

The compartmentalization worked, too. For four days. But by Friday morning the walls started collapsing. Every part of his body, it seemed, had joined in conspiracy against him. Just the thought of coffee sent a surge toward his throat. On the way back to bed he called Bernice's voicemail to say she wouldn't see him that morning, maybe not all day.

Sometime later (he couldn't have said when) a ringing dragged him out of deep sleep and left him floundering on the edge of consciousness. When he finally got hold of his telephone, after knocking it to the floor and hitting his head on the nightstand, he heard Bernice.

"John? Sounds like I woke you. So sorry. I've been debating whether to call."

"It's OK," he croaked. "I had to wake up to answer the phone anyway."

"You still have your sense of humor, whatever that's worth. Don't worry about coming in. I've cancelled your appointments, have things under control."

"I must have the flu or something."

"Most likely *something*."

"What's that mean?"

"We'll talk when you feel better."

"Tell me now. I'll wonder what you meant and won't be able to sleep, and that'll make me sicker."

She paused, considering her response. "No, you need to go back to sleep."

"It might come as a surprise, but I'm still the boss."

"Fine. But remember, this is your idea."

"I'll remember."

"You've been under stress, obviously. I assume it's related to your father. It's made me think about *my* father. He was a shrimper, you know. He had an old boat and a crew of three unreliable characters who preferred to spend their days at Targy's Tavern across from the dock. You sure you're up to this?"

"If you keep it shorter than *War and Peace*."

"Let's not be sarcastic. Anyway, one day Momma saw an ad in the *Times-Picayune* for a seminar on time management and got it in her head that that's what Daddy needed. He wasn't interested, of course. But Momma could pester. She just went at something till she flattened all resistance. And John, I know what you're thinking. Don't you dare say it. So after Momma got a loan from Aunt Mae, Daddy signed up. I was just a little girl, but I remember him standing in front of the mirror before leaving. Momma had bought him a new tie because his was stained with beer from a wedding reception.

"So off he went and two days later came back a time manager, complete with a certificate he framed and hung in the living room, a big three-ring calendar, and a resolve to make every minute productive. In fact, he was so committed he spent most of every morning at the kitchen table planning. Who knows what he was planning? He was supposed to tinker with a diesel engine, mend nets and drag them through the ocean, maybe once in a while scrape barnacles. But he was now so organized he couldn't go to the bathroom without checking his calendar. After a couple of weeks of this,

Momma cooled on the idea of time management. She couldn't get him to stop by the grocery store unless it was on his schedule.

"The positive side, though? He did go down to the dock when his calendar told him to. No matter what. Ever hear of Hurricane Camille? A massive storm, one of the biggest in history. Practically flattened Louisiana. There were warnings. But on the square marked August 17, 1969, Daddy had scheduled an oil change on his boat, and dammit, he wasn't about to let wind stop him! So he went, and what really happened, no one knows. In our family facts weren't as important as the story.

"We heard Daddy's account again and again. We would sit on the floor around his feet as he rolled a cigarette, pausing for effect as he poured tobacco from a white pouch and arranged it in a neat line and licked the edge of the paper. He wouldn't light it till the climax.

"'Daddy,' Nathaniel was expected to ask, 'why'd you go out on that awful day?'

"'Because I had a plan! I was a genu-wine time manager.'

"At this point he'd look up at Momma, who'd shake her head and mutter under her breath, and Daddy would explain how a good boat was like his woman—broad in the beam and a lot of work and too expensive, but generally worth it."

John said, "Ah, Bernice, sorry to interrupt." He now realized how much he had to go the bathroom. "Maybe we ought to get to the part when he lights his cigarette."

"Worried about *War and Peace*, huh? Remember, this was your idea. I'll skip the parts about how he was pulling the dipstick out of the engine when a massive wave struck the boat, causing him to hit his head on the bulkhead, and the next thing he remembered was waking up with a sore head and broken collar bone and his forty foot boat lying on its side, after it took out the front wall of Targy's but thankfully left the bar itself intact, although tragically breaking every bottle in the place, making it impossible to get even a single shot of whiskey for medicinal purposes—really, John, you're missing the best parts of this.

"And then Daddy would put the cigarette in the side of his mouth, and with its end bouncing up and down say, 'And children, what does that go to show?' This was rhetorical, we weren't expected to answer. He'd slowly fish a match out of his pocket and ignite it on the rivet of his jeans and cup it around his cigarette, and he'd squint through the smoke and ask once more, 'Just what does that go to show?' It wasn't our turn yet. 'You can make all the plans you want, you can write 'em down on a twenty-dollar calendar, you can be as organized as Gen'ral Eisenhower hisself on D-Day'—he'd take another drag on his cigarette, holding the smoke for a long while and nodding his head slowly, as if weary with hard-won wisdom—'but you know what? It ain't worth the sweat off a fat lady's—'

"'Willard!' Momma would shout.

"'It ain't worth the sweat off a fat lady's *back*.' He'd flash an aggrieved look at Momma as though that was the word he was going to use all along. 'So what's the moral of this story, children?'

"It was our turn in the liturgy, and we'd respond with the enthusiasm of a congregation happy the service was almost over: '*Things happen.*'

"'That's right,' he'd say with a large sigh, '*things happen.*'"

John said, "This has something to do with me?"

"I think so. Your body knows what I mean, even if you don't. But I've got a call on the other line. Bye for now."

Lying in bed all weekend gave John time to reflect on the things that had happened, and by Sunday morning one more thing happened: everything shifted in his mind, as if a turn of a kaleidoscope created a new picture. After hauling himself downstairs to retrieve newspapers out of the ice plant, he stopped by his desk to pick up the negatives, the first time in a week. They were fixed in his memory, no need to look at them, but—this was when he knew something had changed—he wanted to finger their edges and see if the light shining through one more time would reveal anything new. The pieces of colored glass had fallen into a new design that now commanded his attention.

You win, he thought as he scraped three days of whiskers off his face. *But if you had something to say, why didn't you say it when you were still alive? Afraid of my response? And what the hell am I supposed to do with four-by-five negatives? It's not like I've been storing an enlarger in my closet for something like this.*

As John was cutting a precise edge on his left sideburn a name came to him: Pat Kolwolski. She had been his father's partner in San Diego. They owned a portrait studio, although their primary income came from itinerating through the school district to photograph students. Whenever John heard the name "Pat" or saw a sailboat, he remembered her loud laughter and wild hair flying as she taught him how to sail an Optimist on Mission Bay. His mother thought he was too young (he was eight, maybe nine), but his father said he would be in good hands. Those hands, it turned out, saved his life. They had been on the water about an hour when Pat said, "You take the tiller."

John thrilled at the feel of the dinghy responding to every push and pull, but he pulled too much and the wind knocked the boat over and he sank into a brownish green darkness. Then those good hands grasped under his arms and hauled him up into the light and threw him against the hull to knock out the water, which it did, as well as crack a rib. He started to cry, but Pat laughed all the louder.

"Isn't this fun?" she said, treating the misadventure as part of the lesson. "No big deal, just right the boat and get going again"—a phrase he would repeat to himself when he flubbed a scale or, much later, lost a case. And that's precisely what they did that day, and the next Saturday, too, until he could sail by himself from one end of Mission Bay to the other.

Now he needed her once more. He hadn't talked with her since his parents separated, but by the time he had dried his face and rubbed in aftershave, he was wondering if he could locate her.

Eight

John felt oddly relieved that Pat Kolwolski had an unlisted telephone number and Quality Portraits—if that was still its name—had gone out of business. That meant he would have to drive to San Diego to investigate. This tangible task energized him, perhaps because an unseen part of him caught its breath when he quit running from the past.

By early afternoon on Wednesday he had tossed a toothbrush and change of underwear into the trunk of his Porsche, wrestled a commitment from Joe to rescue his newspapers before the sprinklers started at 6:30 a.m., received blessings from Bernice and Mr. Lambert to be gone a few days, and was now accelerating on the entrance ramp of Interstate 5 in a way that made the $75,000 he paid for his car seem like a bargain.

Near Santa Ana, during an NPR interview with a blues singer, his cellphone rang.

"Hey there," Megan said. "Sorry I missed your call last night. I was out."

Out where? And was that an excuse? She always kept her cellphone with her.

"What's up?" she asked cheerily.

"I guess you've been busy." He waited a few seconds to give her an opportunity to explain. "Just want you to know I'm on my way to San Diego."

"Little vacation?"

"No. Let's say I'm working on those issues that've come between us."

"Good."

"I hope so. And—" He paused, afraid to continue.

"And what?"

"What do you think about getting together this weekend? Maybe Friday, as usual?"

Her silence lasted so long John thought the call had dropped. He started to redial when he heard, "I guess so."

"You don't have to spend the night. I mean, whatever's comfortable. I want to talk, show you something."

"At your place?"

"Yes."

"John, I *have* missed you."

"I've missed you, too."

Over the course of the next hour, John barely noticed the thickening traffic. Nor did he see the ocean at San Juan Capistrano or the hills of Camp Pendleton. His mind had traveled from Megan to another time and place—to a three-bedroom house one block off Balboa Avenue in a middle-class neighborhood in the middle of town. Was it still standing? He saw himself walking up the cracked sidewalk and opening the squeaky screen door and shouting "Mom!" As she came into the living room he would study her face, watching for the droop around her eyes that signaled a change of mood. One afternoon she would tell him his father would not be coming home, and the next afternoon chatter as if nothing had happened, and the next week descend into depression that totally eclipsed life-sustaining warmth. John felt responsible. It was his job to keep the ground as level as possible, a difficult task when the ground beneath his own feet had opened wide.

The old house caused a shock of recognition but nothing more; time had severed the bond of emotion. A crack crawled down its faded yellow stucco and some red tiles from the roof lay strewn on the ground. A German Shepherd patrolled the yard behind a chain-link fence.

After a few minutes John continued his quest, driving four blocks to what had been Quality Portraits. A banner across the front of the building announced the coming of Orchid Thai Restaurant. He peeked through the window and saw scaffolding against the walls and tarps on the floor. Next door was a beauty salon, The Headquarters, where a small Asian woman stood by the entrance, smoking.

She held up the hand not holding a cigarette and said, "You want a manicure?"

"No, thanks."

"Really good job. Only ten dollars."

John shook his head and went inside. The air was heavy with chemicals and blow driers and female laughter. The cashier, her hair a casualty of employee discounts, said Pat Kolwolski had retired about a year ago, sold her house, and bought a boat. She didn't know her current whereabouts. When the cashier threw the question into the room, neither did anyone else, although two hairdressers had heard Pat talk about cruising around the world. That sent speculation cruising around the salon. As John waved goodbye, they agreed that, if she were smart, she would head straight for the Greek Islands and pick up George Clooney on the way.

Finding a sailboat in San Diego is like finding a slot machine in Las Vegas. Where do you begin? The San Diego Yacht Club seemed as good a place as any. Someone there might know her, or have heard about a woman outfitting a boat for a world cruise.

Without lying, strictly speaking, John gave the doorman the impression he was considering membership. He was issued a temporary pass, enabling him to snoop around until he found a bartender who knew Pat. The young man's hair was a suspicious shade of blond, and his biceps, on full display, signaled he could double as a bouncer if necessary. Conversation over wine revealed he had raced J Boats with her. She lived on a thirty-six foot sloop named *Tuesday's Child* berthed at Harbor Island Marina. She was getting ready to sail down the Mexican coast, but maybe she had already left.

Twenty minutes later John inquired at the marina office. He had to make a convincing case that he was neither selling nor soliciting before he learned that *Tuesday's Child* was at the end of Dock H, slip 56: "Dark blue hull, white topsides, can't miss it."

John heard Pat before seeing her. She was offloading opinions about motorboats, good-naturedly it seemed because laughter was ricocheting around the marina. When she saw him she jumped onto the dock and threw her arms around him before he could say anything. She smelled like salt and varnish and sweat.

She held John's at arm's length, studying his face. "My God, boy, you're almost as good-looking as your father."

He wanted to return the compliment but wasn't sure what to say. Her face, set in a huge tangle of white curls, was red, except for fine white lines radiating from each eye. Her nose was covered with a daub of sunscreen, and the skin of her neck changed from crimson to deep brown as it sagged and crevassed its way into a white shirt spotted with paint. Her shorts revealed tanned legs that had accepted no nonsense from age by scrambling atop heaving decks.

"What're you doing here?" she asked. "Come down for another lesson?"

"Afraid not, Captain. May I come aboard?"

"Permission granted," she answered, waving an invitation and pointing to the cockpit bench.

"Pat, I'm not sure what you know about my father—"

"We haven't spoken in years."

"It's been a long time for me, too. But—I'm not sure how to say this—I recently received word he died."

She took a sharp intake of breath and dropped her face into her hands. They did not speak for several minutes.

"What happened?" she asked.

Nine

John told Pat what he knew of his father's death, including a description of his inheritance. "That's one reason I've come to see you. I'm hoping you still have a darkroom."

"I sold my equipment when I retired. But you know, these days plenty of labs do this work digitally."

John knew this. But besides the risk of entrusting strangers with what was an instantly recognizable and possibly valuable negative, there was another reason for asking Pat, one he couldn't easily explain.

"I know," he said. "But it feels right to be with you when I see them."

She nodded. "Let me think a minute." She paused, considering alternatives, and then slapped the boat. "I need to get this gal up to Oceanside for engine work. How 'bout you come with me? We'll sail to Mission Bay, spend the night at Sailboat Cove, and in the morning head up to Oceanside. While they're working on the boat, we'll go to Oceanside Photo. The owner is a friend of mine, Sammy Barnett. He's got a darkroom he'll let us use. What do you say?"

"I didn't exactly pack for a cruise."

"You've got the negatives, don't you?"

"Yes, but—"

"What more do you need?" She looked down at his loafers and said, "I see the problem. So go to The Blue Dolphin, the store next to the marina office, and get some rubber-soled shoes and a sweatshirt. When you're finished with that, go across the street to Ricardo's Market and get a couple of salmon filets for dinner."

John bought canvas sneakers, khaki shorts, and a navy sweatshirt with three pelicans gliding across the chest. And Ricardo, or one of his employees, sold him King salmon "fresh from Alaska." An hour later he was casting off lines as Pat glided *Tuesday's Child* out of the slip.

Turning into the bay Pat pointed the bow directly into the wind and slowed the engine. "Let's sail this boat!" she said. With a mighty heave she pulled a line, and acres of white climbed the mast. With each pull the muscles on her neck grew more distinct. After a final one she said, "There, that'll do it," and she tied the line around a cleat.

"Anything I can do?"

She returned to the wheel and turned off the engine. "You can unfurl the genoa."

As John pulled the line she pointed to, a large foresail rolled from the bow back past the mast, causing the boat to heel sharply. It was unsettling to see water suddenly that close to his body, the more so because his hands were full and not able to hang on.

"Whoa!" he said.

Pat laughed. "Bring back memories, Johnny?"

"The central trauma of my childhood."

"Oh, come on."

He had an urgent problem on his hands, or actually, in his hands; he was still clutching the genoa line and all the wind on earth seemed to be blowing directly into the sail and dragging him toward water churning far too close to his body.

"Pat, what do I do with this?"

"Wrap it around the winch by your shoulder." He started to coil it onto the silver drum, but she said, "No, the other way, clockwise. There you go. In the cubbyhole next to you is a winch handle that'll help get it tighter."

When he finished he crawled to the high side of the boat. Ragged clouds above and white chop beneath scudded across a world of blue. About a dozen other boats were out, along with gulls and cormorants and pelicans. A red buoy bobbed with the waves; on its base three seals sunbathed and slept, undisturbed by the clanging bell, and at its waterline mussels and barnacles congregated with abandon.

"Look," Pat said, pointing to a naval installation. "Submarines. They give me the creeps." Her hair was a long mane, blowing straight back. "And there's Point Loma. We'll round it and head north to Mission Bay."

In open water the chop turned to swells, and John remembered why he had retired from sailing shortly after mastering the Optimist. His queasiness must have registered on his face because Pat nodded toward the cabin and told him where to find ginger tablets.

The companionway steps led down to a chamber of rocking torment. He found the ginger as quickly as possible and climbed back into fresh air with the urgency of a diver out of oxygen.

Pat said, "Time to come about, mate. You tend the genoa as we go hard to starboard."

"English, please."

"Release the rope around the winch when I turn right."

"Aye, aye."

With one hand she spun the wheel and with the other she loosed the mainsail. He released the genoa into a furious flapping. As the boat crossed the wind, it heeled hard to the right, throwing him to the opposite side of the cockpit.

"Beautiful," Pat said. "A fine team. Here, you take the wheel."

He didn't want the wheel or anything else to do with her boat. But before he could express himself, Pat went forward to coil a loose halyard. That left him little choice. He tried to keep *Tuesday's Child* on course until she returned. But when she did, she sat next to him, content to let him steer.

He began to relax a little, even to enjoy the ride. He found the rhythm: a wave's push against the bow and then the trough's pull, a puff of wind and then the correction, and thinking of these things got his mind off his stomach. And this thinking eventually ventured into the surrounding spaciousness, the sea's vastness. He had been a festival of self-absorption. But then the ocean: its magnitude reduced him to an inconsequential speck, and it was a relief. He kept taking deep breaths, not for more oxygen but for more immensity.

John was jolted out of reverie when Pat said, "Damn!" She took off her large sunglasses, revealing red eyes and wet cheeks. "I loved him, you know." Perhaps she wanted to say more but couldn't find the words.

The sun slid seaward and its softening light skipped across the summit of the waves, laying a golden carpet that led directly to their boat. As they neared buoys marking the entrance to Mission Bay, Pat said, "Well done, Johnny. But you'd better let me take over."

Soon orders flew and John struggled to remember the difference between sheets and halyards. Pat started the engine, the genoa furled onto the forestay, the mainsail fell to the boom, and they glided into Sailboat Cove, an enclave that seemed especially still after the open sea.

Pat said, "It's about time to drop the hook and pop a cork, don't you think?"

Ten

As John ignited coals in the grill attached to the stern railing, his imagination flared with movie scenes of boats exploding and he hoped, after motoring into Sailboat Cove, no fumes were lingering around them. Pat didn't act worried as she poured Pinot Noir into crystal stemware, surprisingly elegant for the circumstances, and lifted her glass for a toast.

"Here's to Logan Stanhope," she said with a voice losing its hold on the crumbling ledge of composure.

"Tell me about him," he said.

She looked into his eyes for a few seconds, as if weighing something, and then cleared a place to sit amidst damp lines and discarded sweatshirts.

"We weren't lovers," she said. "Might as well get that out of the way in case you were wondering." She stretched a leg to rest her foot on the bottom of the wheel. "We were friends, good friends. But sorry to say, we haven't talked in years. The occasional phone calls when he moved north were awkward—maybe that's too strong. My fault, I suppose. Feelings of abandonment."

"I'm familiar with those feelings. Where did you meet?"

"At Cal. Let's see, it would've been fall of '62. We happened to sit next to each other in Introduction to Philosophy. Through Plato and Aristotle we smiled and said 'Hi.' During Descartes your father whispered, 'I drink, therefore I am. Want to help affirm my existence?' By the linguistic analysts we considered ourselves friends, though we had long discussions about whether the word 'friend' signified any reality outside the utterance of it. You know, typical undergraduate bullshit."

Pat took another swallow of wine and gazed across the bay, almost squinting, as if struggling to see a barely visible past. As she described their friendship, John's mind occasionally wandered, not from boredom but from a surfeit of stimulation; every sentence reverberated and echoed and called up his own memories—comments from his father and mother, especially—and he tried to stitch it all together into a sensible narrative.

Pat and Logan had come from different worlds. She was reared in Berkeley, the eldest of three children. Her father, Dr. Karl Kolwolski, was a professor at the University of California and her mother an architect. Pat learned she could hold any opinion, as long as she supported it with reasonable arguments; the only sin was indifference. Her family was "vaguely Unitarian, excuse the redundancy," which meant it wasn't long before Pat and Logan crossed swords, his father being an Episcopal bishop, a chaplain to the establishment she had been taught to distrust. He planned to return east after graduation to uphold the Stanhope tradition of attending Episcopal Divinity School in Massachusetts. Accordingly, he majored in philosophy to prepare for the family business.

But in his junior year he took a course from Dr. Kolwolski—"The Causes and Consequences of Poverty." Something started churning inside him that was part of a larger churning: the previous year President Kennedy had been shot and Martin Luther King Jr. had led his march on Washington; Mario Savio made speeches in Sproul Plaza and the university president, Clark Kerr, had had 800 students arrested. The cultural foundations were cracking. Seeping through the fissures were hopes for a more just society.

"One day," she said, "we were studying in Bancroft Library, sitting at the same table. He was writing a paper for Dad's class and went to find a book. Didn't come back for, I don't know, maybe two hours! I thought he'd gone to his dorm for a nap or something. When he finally showed up he was carrying a pile of oversized books. Seems he'd discovered the photography section. After that, nothing was the same for him—or for me. He might've passed his classes that semester but I wouldn't bet on it. He was always hanging out with Lange and Adams and Weston and Cunningham.

"Once I saw him on a bench near Sather Gate. He had one of the books on his lap, oblivious to everything else. I snuck up behind him and peeked over his shoulder. A Weston nude.

"'So,' I said, 'you've come to this prestigious academy to ogle women!'

"He turned around and gave me that expression of his—the twinkling eyes, the smile of a six-year-old about to do something naughty.

"'Look,' he said, as he turned over a few pages to one of Weston's Point Lobos rocks and then flipped back and forth between the two. 'See the similarities? The form, the composition?' I told him I didn't see much similarity between a wet rock and a bare ass. He rolled his eyes in disgust but escorted me through the book like a docent. He was mesmerized by rock formations and cypress groves and tree stumps. 'The thing is,' he said, 'Weston *saw* what most people walk by.'

"But Dorothea Lange really got to him. Her pictures of Oakies and other poor souls touched him deeply. People on the edge of survival were a world away—actually, a *universe* away—from his upbringing. She showed the defeated shoulders and abused hands and rutted faces of poverty.

"He wanted to see it for himself. The university had begun experimenting with alternative learning options, so in his senior year your father proposed a research project: he would document the life of farmworkers in the San Joaquin Valley—do interviews, make observations, write a report. This was *Berkeley*, after all. Social research was all the rage. So of course his advisor agreed. What didn't they agree to, if a student was earnest enough?

"Anyway, about a week before he left he came to our house for dinner. By then he was no stranger to my family, and he had pretty much learned to hold his own in the verbal fisticuffs around our table. The conversation that evening wandered into modern art, particularly photography, and Dad was making the case that Cartier-Bresson was, so far, the premier photographer of the twentieth century, that no one had approached his genius for capturing human experience. Logan questioned this, offering Lange as a contrary example, and Dad swung back, contending that her work was too stylized, too much like set-pieces.

"'Her characters are on stage,' he said, 'but Cartier-Bresson's, you hear their breathing, smell their sweat.'

"And then Dad suddenly slammed his palms on the table, pushed back his chair, and left the room. The rest of us looked at each other with surprise. It wasn't like him to abandon a fight without more bloodshed. But after a few minutes he returned, placed a camera in front of Logan, and said, 'Here. Take it with you to Bakersfield. Let's see what you can do.'

"Logan stared at the camera as if it were a stick of dynamite. Usually, he had a natural confidence—almost cockiness—but he was unhinged. Just sat there, stunned. He didn't know what to do or say.

"Dad said, 'It's a Leica M3. I bought it a few years ago on sabbatical in Germany.'

"Logan didn't need anyone to tell him about Leicas. He'd been haunting camera stores in Berkeley, dreaming and scheming. He coughed and drank water, trying not to cry. He said he couldn't, that the offer was kind but he didn't want the responsibility. To which Dad dismissively waved his hand and said, 'Nonsense. It's just collecting dust. You might as well put it to use. Return it with pictures that tell us something.'

"Those were his exact words. *Return it with pictures that tell us something.* I didn't think much about it. But your father did. Oh yeah.

"And he started that semester. In the fields and small towns of the Valley he learned not only about farmworkers but how to see through a rangefinder and how to make images that told the truth and conveyed what he felt. That little camera became his constant companion, an extension of himself."

Eleven

Soft light shone from cabins of other boats swinging at anchor in the cove, and sounds of laughter and splashing travelled easily on the evening air. John had been assigned the salmon, which he eyed like a hungry gull until he became distracted by another sailboat. The light atop its mast flashed glimpses of what appeared to be swimmers without benefit of swimsuits. He imagined, with a stab of longing, skinny dipping with Megan. Pat broke his reverie and saved the fish from a sad fate by hollering that she was ready whenever he was.

The galley's table had been set with salad, warm bread, and another bottle of wine.

"*Bon appetit*, John."

"Good to be here. Shouldn't have waited so long."

She held up a hand like a policeman stopping cars. "Let's not go down that road. I'm done with *should have* and *shouldn't have*. What matters is now—and here we are, together again."

The lantern cast a warm glow into the cabin. Pat told of her upcoming trip down the coast and her plans to sail to New Zealand and Australia, and she listed the stops on her itinerary, in great detail it seemed to John, until her words smoothed into a lullaby to accompany the rocking womb of *Tuesday's Child*.

He woke when his head bounced against the wall. The table had been cleared, and Pat was washing dishes, humming softly to herself. He stretched and groaned and massaged stiffness out of his neck.

"At least you didn't spill the wine when you conked out."

"I'm lousy company."

"You're not the first man I've put to sleep. Ready for decaf?"

"Sure."

"What do you say we go topside again?"

"Good."

"You'll probably need that new sweatshirt."

The air—bracing after the cabin—revived John. The night was a black dress sequined with stars and city lights.

"So Dad went to Bakersfield?"

"Right. From your perspective, his most important discovery was Aimee Coles."

"Lucky for me. Not so much for her."

"I could have strangled her with jealousy. I didn't believe it would work. Her father, an appliance repairman, and her mother, a half-crazed Pentecostal evangelist? Can you imagine how far that was from your father's world? But you must know all this."

"No, continue."

"She had dropped out of Bakersfield Community College to work in her mother's ministry, part of which involved distributing boxed lunches to migrants. By then, I guess, your father had imbibed my father's egalitarianism, maybe got a little drunk on it. Overlooking their differences was part of the attraction, if you ask me. But I'm no psychologist. Anyway, they fell in love and by Christmas were engaged to be married, against the wishes of both sets of parents.

"The week after commencement my family drove to the wedding. What a scene! Lordy! Did your parents ever talk about it?"

"Not that I remember."

"The Right Reverend and Mrs. John McIntyre Stanhope—your esteemed and oh-so-cultured grandparents—seated in a Foursquare chapel on the outskirts of Bakersfield: one in a purple shirt with clerical collar, the other in a silk suit that probably came from Saks Fifth Avenue, witnessing their son's marriage by your other grandmother—a woman who began the ceremony with a message in tongues and ended it with a call for healing. Your father liked to say that a cotton picker with a bad back went forward for the laying-on of hands, but the only miracle was that his parents didn't faint.

"Logan's decision to stay in Bakersfield would've been bad enough, but they were especially pissed that he turned his back on the priesthood. The first in who-knows-how-many generations of Stanhopes. Snapping pics wasn't saving souls. But Chavez offered him a small stipend to return to the camps and photograph conditions, and Dad helped make that possible by giving him the Leica as a wedding gift."

"So what were you doing?"

"I was upset that Dad gave away his Leica! Hanging around your father got me interested in photography. And what else could I do with a degree in philosophy? My parents wanted me to get a PhD, but I had had enough of academics. When I made a case for photography—which meant doing my homework, marshalling arguments, and even, this is the truth, producing a flip chart that proved something or other—they disagreed but, true to form, supported me all the way and insisted I get the best education possible. So I enrolled at Brooks Institute in Santa Barbara.

"Occasionally Logan and I talked on the phone, though neither of us could afford it. Most of the time we exchanged letters, discussing and debating. Remember, this was the sixties. Photography, as he saw it, was a way to help people see the oppression and violence that seemed woven into the fabric of America."

"You disagreed?"

"I believed it could make a difference. Images touch emotions like maybe nothing else. But for me, photography was essentially art. What's the point of art? To preach sermons? I don't think so. Art has its own purposes, should be judged by its own standards. Ideologies pretty quickly hijack the enterprise. It's an old argument. Eventually, by the way, your father came around to my view. But after—"

"Vietnam?"

"Yes, Vietnam." Pat stood and leaned against the boom. "Your father had come across the Korean War pictures of David Douglas Duncan, and he got the notion that to make it as a photojournalist he needed to cover our war. On the basis of his work with migrants, Time-Life offered to look at what he sent them. No salary, just the name of an editor. Your mom was now pregnant, but your father promised to be home before you were born. She moved in with her parents, and he headed to Saigon.

"I don't know what happened over there. Early on he wrote a few letters with news he had sold something. One photo made the cover of *Time*. But his letters got shorter and—I'm not sure how to describe it—"

"Did he talk about it when he returned?"

"Never. He built a wall around the experience, hung a 'No Trespassing' sign on it." Pat was staring into the darkness, as if it contained the mystery. "I think he went over there to tell the truth, the whole of it—the fear, the

confusion, the death. They say 'the truth shall set you free.' Maybe. But before that, it can damn near kill you.

"He returned six months later, in time for your arrival, and spent
the next year working for a painting contractor. Meanwhile, I finished at
Brooks and, with backing from my parents, took over a portrait business in
San Diego. I ended up signing a contract with the school district to do class
pictures—not art, but a way to pay bills. It was a big job and I needed help,
so I invited—begged, really—your father to join me. He had zero interest in
squirming kids, but he was eager to escape the in-laws, so he packed up his
family and moved down here."

Pat threw the last of her coffee overboard. "Enough for now," she said.
"This old lady is off to bed. I'm set up in the aft cabin, so you take the
forward." She bent over and kissed John on the forehead. "See you in the
morning."

Twelve

John woke before the sun had climbed into a new day. Through a small oval window he could see, in predawn light, the world slumbering on, save a gull with rooster aspirations. He dreaded exchanging the warmth of bed for the chill of the head, but negotiations with his bladder had come to an end.

When he finished, Pat was in the galley wearing a floral-print swimsuit with a white towel wrapped around her waist.

"G'morning, mate," she said. "Sleep well?"

"Very."

She pointed to the shower. "Help yourself. I prefer the bay. If you want to join me, these might fit." She held out a pair of men's trunks, bright red. "Don't ask, it's a long story."

"As much fun as it'd be to wear a stranger's swimsuit, I'll try the shower."

John bumped and bruised himself in a cubby that reeked of plastic and bilge water. He managed to get relatively dry before dressing, and then he filled the largest mug he could find, climbed into a bright morning, and stretched out on the cockpit bench.

Pat was still in the water, about fifty yards out, cavorting like a dolphin the first week of creation. She would jackknife, plunging head down, lifting her large rump into the air, pointing feet toward the sky, and disappearing into the depths. A minute later she would burst up again, rising high and streaming with water. When she saw him she waved and swam back toward the boat.

Tranquility penetrated the cove as deeply as oil into the grain of teak; primordial quietness had tiptoed across the water, crept into every boat, crawled under every granule of sand. Silence reigned, and lapping water and even gulls seemed to serve the realm. The water, except Pat's wake, mirrored with precision everything on its surface or around its shore.

What would the day bring? That's what John wondered as coffee slid down his throat and sun warmed his face. What would the pictures tell him?

Pat hauled herself up the stern ladder and said quietly, almost reverently, "Now that's the way to begin a day." She dried and faced the sun, standing motionless, holding the towel against her chest, her eyes meditatively closed, as if praying the rays into every pore of her face. Slowly she turned toward John and said, "More coffee?"

"Sure, thanks."

She took his mug and a few seconds later returned it full. "Ready for breakfast?"

"Anytime."

Crackling bacon soon sent an aroma toward him that won a space for grace amidst sodium and cholesterol, and each salivary gland became a cataract of desire that swept him down into the cabin. He ate more than was prudent, considering the swells to come.

Pat said it was time to "haul stern" before the day got away from them. So John washed dishes and she scurried about topside, removing sail covers and coiling sheets and cranking up the diesel.

They motored until midmorning when a steady onshore breeze filled the sails and lifted the boat into a sweet spot that necessitated no tacking or coming about or any of the lunging and ducking that made John long for dry land. Pat seemed to have drained herself of memories; she was clearly comfortable with silence, a fortunate trait, John thought, in someone about to sail around the world by herself.

That afternoon, approaching Oceanside Harbor, Pat radioed Brewster's Mechanical to signal their approach, and they were met at the dock by a man covered in grease. John tossed him the bow line too hard, forcing the man to duck as he tried to catch it. John overcompensated with the stern line, this time hitting the water; Pat chuckled and Grease Man shook his head.

"Good help is hard to find," Pat said.

"Shouldn't be hard to find *better* help," Grease Man said with no indication he was trying to be funny.

In the office Pat said something about through-hull fittings, signed a work order, and persuaded the manager to lend them a beat-up Suburban, which they drove to Oceanside Photo on Highway 101 next to a Harley Davidson store. Pat had to wedge it between a delivery truck and a chrome-laden, cherry-red motorcycle, whose owner—wearing an open leather vest that displayed a chest full of snakes and long-haired women—was not smiling. Pat managed, with considerable turning of wheels and shifting of gears, to get next to the curb without incident. John thought it best to disappear as quickly as possible, while Pat sauntered by the biker, winked, and said, "Nice wheels."

Sammy Barnett was busy with a customer but motioned toward the darkroom. They selected a packet of printing paper, eleven by fourteen inches, before entering a small room thick with the stench of chemicals but clean enough for surgery. A workbench against one wall held an enlarger and three trays; a shelf attached to the opposite wall held drying racks and brown bottles and yellow boxes.

Pat checked the enlarger's lenses and found a box of filters. She filled the trays with developer and stop bath and fixer. After turning on the red safety light, she turned off the overhead light.

"All right," she said. "We're ready. How about a negative?"

John's eyes hadn't adjusted to the dimness, but from what he could tell, he handed her the one that looked completely dark. It was impossible to recognize anything on the easel, until she lifted the lens up into the bellows to enlarge the picture to the dimensions of the paper, and then, with a magnifying glass, found a detail on which to sharpen the focus.

After experimenting with different exposures on a test strip, she said, "Let's try twelve seconds at f/11. Here goes."

About fourteen seconds later she placed the paper in the developer.

"You ready for this?" she asked.

John's face was wet and his jaw clenched.

Thirteen

S lowly, details began to emerge on the shiny wet paper. A horizon line, rocks, maybe some bushes. Was that sage? And what was that in the lower right corner? A tripod?

Fourteen

A thermometer on a bank building in Barstow said 102. It must be ten degrees hotter by now. We're heading north from the Mojave Desert toward Death Valley so Dad can photograph property for someone. He's driving the old boat, our green '62 Oldsmobile 88. A furnace is blasting through open windows. We'll shut them soon and then suffocate. It's hard to decide what's worse, so we go back and forth. A map lies on my legs, flapping in the wind. I'm the navigator. I'm tired of sitting but not going to mention it. Mom said I was too young to be dragged through the desert, but Dad said nonsense, twelve was plenty old enough, and besides it would be fun to have me along. I don't want to disappoint him.

Dad says, "Looks like we're driving into water, doesn't it?"

"Why's it doing that?"

"Sunlight reflects off hot air rising from the pavement."

When we see a gas station—Weaver's Gas and Oil—Dad stops because it might be the last one for many miles. Two faded red pumps stand on a slab of cement as cracked as Grandpa's face before he died. Or maybe it's still cracked, depending. I've been wondering what he looks like now, lying in the dark, underground. Sometimes at night I think about stuff like this and it keeps me awake. A small gray building sits next to them; in one window is a sign for Camel cigarettes and in the other a large cardboard bottle of Coke.

Dad says, "Want something to drink?"

"Sure."

A man in a shirt the color of Mom's dusting rags, with patches of sweat under each armpit, walks slowly from the building. The bottom half of his face, covered with stubble, looks like cactus. The rest of his head is bald, shiny where there aren't moles, and his face droops like a sad dog's. He's gnawing a large wad of something, tobacco I guess, because disgusting juice is running down the side of his chin.

He walks around to Dad's window and leans down. "Fill 'er up?"

"Premium, please." The man starts pumping gas and Dad says, "Pretty warm, huh?"

"Hotter'n hell on a bad day."

"Got some Coke in there?"

"Yep. Help yourself."

Dad jerks his head toward the building. "Go ahead, Johnny. Get me one, too."

The screen door squeaks as I push it open, and when I let go, it slams hard, loud enough to resurrect a dead dog, not to mention a sleeping one. On my right, growling warns me not to take another step. Not that I could anyway with my body frozen stiff.

The man hollers, "Don't worry! Buster's too hot to bite anyone!"

My eyes take a minute to adjust to the dark, and then I see a large black creature lying next to the Coke box—a red tub-like refrigerator with a top that swings open. I'm not thirsty anymore. But Dad is, and I don't want to admit I'm afraid, so I have to keep walking toward Coke and Buster. I've never heard of a dog being too hot to bite, and I can't forget what happened about a year ago when I did Dave Bronson's paper route for him and a Boxer came running around the side of the house and attacked me, or actually my bag, growling and tearing *The San Diego Union* to shreds before his owner pulled him off and said, "Sorry, he's really nice," which is something I've noticed dog owners always say. That's why I'm watching Buster closely, pretending I'm not scared. And he's watching me, following my every step.

"Hey fella," I say, friendly like. "That's a good boy."

He growls again, but half-heartedly, more out of duty than conviction.

I keep walking until I reach the red tub. My foot is now within striking distance of his teeth. Help me, Jesus. I open the top and pull two bottles out of ice water, and when I turn to retreat, Buster jumps up and barks like he's going to kill me.

I wet my pants.

Just then the screen door opens. "Shut up you crazy beast! He's loud but won't hurt you."

I don't say anything because I'm concentrating on squeezing muscles down there, trying to stop peeing.

Dad follows the man to the cash register, and I quickly hand off a bottle to get outside before pee leaks into my jeans. Now I'm grateful for the heat. Instead of going back to the car, I walk around as bow-legged as I can, and I keep looking down for evidence. The water hose next to the air hose gives me an idea. I sit on a ledge by the pumps and fake a big swig of Coke, carefully spilling some on my lap. "Shoot!" I say, in a loud voice, setting the bottle down. I pull the water hose off its roller and start spraying my crotch.

Dad and the man come back outside at that moment, and Dad says, "What the Sam Hill you doing?"

"I spilled some Coke. Thought I better rinse it off."

Dad says, "Well, now—"

The man finishes his sentence, "Looks like you pissed your pants."

They both laugh, and I join them, as if that would be the funniest thing in the world.

The man asks, "What're you doing out this way?"

Dad says, "Headed up the road a few miles for business. I'm a photographer."

"What're you shooting?"

"Property my client's thinking of buying."

"What else you shoot?"

"Pretty much everything. You go where jobs are, you know."

"Everything?" The man seems surprised. He shakes his head and spits a long yellowish-brown stream that lands next to his foot. "*Everything.*" This time it isn't a question, just a statement. "I've got a lot to learn."

"You interested in photography?"

"I take some pictures." The man motions with his hand for us to follow him. Dad glances at my soaking-wet crotch, and nods his head in the direction the man is walking. I trail behind them, thinking it was a dumb idea to spray myself. My jeans and underpants are sticking to me, and I put my hands in my pockets, trying to pull the wet denim away from my body.

Behind the station, there's something strange: a tripod, with camera on its head, and an umbrella attached to it for shade. And the weirdest thing is the legs of the tripod are planted in a tub of hard, dry sand.

Dad says, "I've seen a lot of tripods but never set up like that."

"No point moving it till I'm finished."

The camera is aimed at nothing but rocks and a few bushes.

Dad's eyes are focused in the same direction as the camera. Then he looks down at me with a blank expression, as if he has no idea what to say.

Again he studies the scene the man is photographing, and looks back at me, this time shrugging his shoulders and rolling his eyes slightly.

The man says, "Let me show you something," and walks to an old trailer, not large, set up on cinderblocks. Three metal steps lead to a small door he opens.

Inside, prints are everywhere—on walls, stacked in piles—and there are hundreds, maybe thousands. They're all the same scene, and each one has a label, such as "January 12, 1975, 9:10 AM," or "January 13, 1975, 10:20 AM," and so on. Some have blank sky, some clouds; some have puffy clouds, some stringy; some are blinding white, some nearly black; some have long shadows next to rocks, some short shadows.

Dad says nothing, only shakes his head.

The man says, "So much happening out there."

Not enough to keep me interested. I'm ready to hit the road again, especially now that my pants are almost dry. But Dad is in no hurry, taking his time, still not talking. Inside the trailer it's as hot as an oven. It might be better outside, so I start down the steps—until Buster comes sniffing around the trailer. I'd rather be baked than eaten, so back I go. But the dog reminds me of peeing, which makes me realize I *do* need to pee, not because of fear this time but because Buster didn't scare it all out of me and it's been a long drive and I drank a Coke, or most of it.

"May I use the bathroom?"

"Number one or two?"

"Just one."

He makes a sweeping gesture, as if to say the whole desert is my toilet.

That would be fine, no problem. Except for Buster. I imagine somehow getting by him and walking around the side of the trailer and unzipping my pants, and just imagining this makes me need to go even more, so much so it almost starts then and there, until I also imagine Buster biting me in a very painful spot.

I point to the dog. "Will he . . . ?"

"Nope. Won't hurt you."

I've heard that before.

Dad seems unaware of our conversation. Just keeps looking at the pictures. He has a print in both hands and is studying one on the wall. Eventually, as I'm doing a fidgety dance, he frees his right hand and reaches toward the man, saying, "I'm Logan Stanhope."

The man shakes it and says, "Weaver. Bill Weaver. Glad to meet you."

"The pleasure is mine. Really. Listen, if it's all right, I'd like to take my own picture of this scene." Mr. Weaver nods, and Dad goes outside to get his gear, with me following closely.

I explain my problem.

Dad smiles. "Now that you mention it, I need to go, too."

We walk over to a clump of sage. Mine is tiny next to Dad's but shoots farther into the sage than his.

When we finish Dad gets his camera and tripod out of the car, surveys the scene by pacing back and forth several times, and then settles on a spot just behind the man's tripod.

Mr. Weaver comes up beside him and says, "Nice camera. Four-by-five?"

"Yeah. Makes a nice negative."

"Linhof, huh?"

Dad nods. "Can't beat the Germans."

"They know how to make glass, for sure."

Dad focuses his lens and says, "If only the photographer was as good as the camera."

"Yep. Got the same problem."

When we're finally on our way, I'm happy to be leaving Weaver's Gas and Oil, especially Weaver's dog. The property Dad has to photograph turns out to be a rocky patch of desert just like everything around it. The temperature must be 120 degrees in the shade, except there's no shade for a hundred miles in every direction. Everything—car seat, door handle, dirt outside—is a burning misery. We both want to get back to San Diego.

The rest of the day Dad says little. Darkness brings some relief from heat; it's still hot, but now you can almost stand it. Dad's left arm hangs out the window, and the wind makes his hairs stand upright. Lights from oncoming cars show stubble appearing on his face, not like Mr. Weaver's yet, but enough for me to wonder when I'll have a beard. My chin feels hopelessly smooth.

Dad is so quiet I'm worried he knows I wet my pants. I'm afraid to say anything but decide to chance it. "Are you mad?"

He jumps, as if startled. "Oh no. Sorry, son. You've been great—terrific navigator and assistant. No, I've been thinking about that Weaver fellow at the station. Can't get him out of my mind. And his pictures."

Fifteen

Pat pressed on, placing the next negative in the enlarger and position-ing its image on the white easel. After adjusting the focus, she turned off the enlarger's light, slid another piece of paper on the easel, and again exposed it for twelve seconds.

As the paper lay in the developer, we saw trees gradually take shape on both sides, and toward the bottom, what appeared to be a trail.

Sixteen

We're in the Mountain View Diner in Lone Pine, a small town on the eastern side of the Sierra. On the knotty pine wall above our booth are faded pictures of guys in cowboy hats, and next to them, pictures of maybe the same guys galloping after Indians through sage brush and huge rocks. Dad points out Gene Autry and Roy Rogers, and when he sees I don't know who they are, tells me they were famous when he was a kid.

I recognize John Wayne and Clint Eastwood. "I wonder if they ate here."

"Maybe."

It's my fourteenth birthday. Dad brought me here to spend the night and have an all-day hike tomorrow. He wants it to be fun for me, since we're celebrating my being born and all, but he's also excited about taking pictures along the Mount Whitney Trail. He's sick of doing portraits, and lately he's been going on and on about getting to his real work.

I'm fiddling with the saltshaker as we wait for our hamburgers.

"Fourteen years old," Dad says, slapping open palms on the table. "Growing up."

I shrug my shoulders, not sure what to say.

"Too old for toys, I suppose." Dad rummages around in a bag next to him, pulls out a gift in bright red paper, and hands it to me. "Happy birthday, son."

I glance around the restaurant, hoping nobody is watching. Mom must have wrapped the package because it's too neat for him to have done it himself. Whenever Dad and I try to wrap presents, it's pretty funny. Mom says they're beautiful but we know it's not true. I slip my finger under the tape to save the paper the way Mom likes, but Dad waves his hand and says, "Come on, rip into it!"

What I thought was a box is actually a shiny brown leather case, a little nicked-up, and inside is a camera with two lenses, one above the other.

"That's no Brownie," he says. "It's a Rollicord, a fine piece of equipment. A little bulky, I know, but you're going to like the big negatives in the darkroom." He shows me how the hood pops up. "That's the focusing screen."

I'm practically speechless. Right off, I know what it means. I'm old enough to do what he loves. All I can come up with is, "Wow, thanks," and I keep repeating it.

The waitress brings our hamburgers and says, "Looks like somebody's got a birthday."

"My son here is fourteen."

"No way," she says, looking not at me but at Dad. "You can't be old enough to have a teenager." You'd have to be blind not to see her flirting with him. Believe me, she's not the first. Mom says they can't keep their eyes off him. He's handsome, I guess, though you don't really think of your Dad that way. Maybe you'd notice if he were ugly. I don't know.

I study him with scientific eyes, the way Mr. Jacobsen said we were supposed to examine the guts of a dead frog. Of course it would be dead if we dissected it. Anyway, I notice his hair is wilder than usual because we've had the windows open on the drive up here. A piece of it curls down over his forehead, so bright in the sunlight it's almost white. His eyes are supposed to be the big deal, if you count the number of compliments they get. They're blue, bluer than the sky behind him. The lines around his mouth are like a couple of parentheses, the left one so deep you wonder what might be in it, and his smile is as crooked as the back leg of our neighbor's dog. The freckles on his nose worry me that mine won't be fading anytime soon. So what do women like, exactly? Hard to say, not being one.

"You look familiar," she says. "Here to film a movie?"

"Nope. To hike."

"Well, you *could* be an actor."

She winks at him, touches his shoulder, and walks back to the kitchen in a way that makes her bottom move like two pistons, one side up and the other down, bump bump, bump bump, in regular rhythm, and to tell the truth, it's hard not to watch. When we turn back toward each other, we both have a guilty smile.

59

Reaching for the ketchup I say, "Women love you," and before the words are out of my mouth, I'm embarrassed.

"No, not really. Some like the way I look. And from what I can tell, you're going to have the same problem, if you want to call it that. Before long, they'll be making eyes at you. But remember, just because they look at you doesn't mean they see you. Know what I mean? Women like what they imagine about me but that's different from liking me. You understand what I'm saying?"

Personally, I'd be happy either way, girls looking at me or seeing me. But I nod my head and say, "Yeah."

Several times during our meal the waitress stops by our booth to see how we're doing, to fill our water glasses, to be around Dad. When she clears our plates she says, "You guys leave any room for dessert?"

Dad says, "I'll bet you can find us some apple pie with a scoop of vanilla. And how about two cups of coffee?" As if two adults are sitting here. When the coffee comes I do my best not to make a face when I swallow it.

In our room at the Sierra Vista Motel, Dad motions for me to sit next to him on the bed. Holding my camera he says, "I thought it would be better to get a used one instead of a piece of crap." He smiles. If Mom were here, he'd be in trouble for saying "crap," but tonight it's just us and that's why he's smiling. "If you're going to take pictures, you'd better learn how to run this thing."

He shows me how to open and focus it, and tells me to be careful with the lens, not to scratch it, as if I didn't know that, and says he needs to teach me the basics of photography. I must look scared because he says, "Don't worry, you'll get the hang of it."

In his camera bag, sitting on the other side of him, he finds a light meter.

"Here, we need to start with this. It's an extra one you can have. Photography is all about light. With each exposure, each snap of the shutter, we let in light. The more it touches the film, the darker the negative, which means the lighter the print. Following me?"

Without waiting for an answer, he keeps going.

"But how much should we let in? That's the crucial question, which is why we need a meter. It measures the amount of light. See this red button here? If you push it, the needle jumps and gives you a reading. It shows the various options you've got for shutter speeds and f-stops."

Now I'm totally lost, and he knows it. So he explains it again and again, like Mom trying to squeeze our car into a small space, coming at it from different angles until the idea is more or less parked in my brain. Eventually I understand there are two variables: as one changes so must the other, and knowing how to do this separates photographers from snapshot shooters. In our family snapshot shooters have as much respect as dog poop.

"The faster the shutter speed," I repeat after him, "the faster the action I can stop. So if somebody's walking I would use 1/125 of a second, but if somebody's running, 1/250?"

"You've got it. And if you want to stop a moving car, you'd use 1/500."

"What about a bullet? Could I stop a bullet?"

"Not unless it hit your camera."

"And the faster the shutter speed, the lower the f/stop number has to be—"

"Because?"

"A lower f/stop is a larger opening to let in more light, right?"

"Right. A setting of f/2.8 is a larger aperture (the technical term) than, say, f/16."

"Does the size of the *aperture*"—I say the word slowly, emphasizing every syllable, to prove that I've been listening—"make any difference?"

"Great question! Yes, this is *really* important. The lower the f/stop number (2.8, for example, or 4), the shallower your depth of field. The higher the number (16 or 22), the greater your depth of field."

"What's depth of field?"

"The area in focus. Look at that lamp in front of the window. Now look at the mountain through the window. You can't focus on both at the same time, can you? Humans see with a shallow depth of field. Cameras are different. They can see everything at once, get everything in focus. Of course you may not always want that. Sometimes it's nice to have a blurry background. The f/stops give you that control. So if you want to have only the lamp in focus and everything behind it blurry, you would set your camera at f/2.8. On the other hand, if you want both the lamp and the mountain sharp, you would set it at f/22. It's easy to remember: the lower the number, the less in focus, and the higher the number, the more in focus. Got it?"

I nod, but am sure I'll forget it by tomorrow.

"And you can't do much without film," Dad says. He reaches into his camera bag and pulls out a large yellow box. "Here's the rest of your present.

Ten rolls of Tri-X. It's grainier than I prefer, but also faster and gives more flexibility in dark areas, like the forest."

Faster? I imagine my film on the track at school, beating all the other rolls in a race. I don't ask what he means because I've had enough of the basics of photography and am ready for bed.

The next morning, before light, we drive west on Whitney Portal Road to the trailhead parking lot. About twenty cars are already there. Dad says this is one of the most popular trails in California, the route climbers take to ascend the highest peak in America, not counting Alaska. I've never seen anything like it. The mountain rises steeply out of the desert, and this morning, being the middle of May, snow still blankets it, making it even more amazing as the sun, not yet lighting the valley, sets the peak on fire.

I try to think about how beautiful the mountain is, how it's maybe even proof of God, how lucky I am to be here—I work at keeping these good thoughts because I sense another one creeping toward me, an unclean one, as if it's crouching down and ready to pounce. And sure enough, it does. The mountain looks like a giant breast, the way it rises up on all sides. And we're going to hike up it! Like bugs crawling toward the nipple. And if these thoughts aren't bad enough, if I'm not already in big enough trouble with God, another one is creeping up on me, and the harder I try to keep it away the closer it gets, a dirty word I don't want to let into my mind but can't stop, and then it pounces—*tit*. The mountain is a giant tit. I'm a filthy rag, a vile sinner. I've given in to the impure thoughts Brother Wally warned about in his talk to the boys when the girls went with Sister Eleanor. I want to be clean, I really do, a pure vessel for the Holy Spirit, but here I am thinking about tits, and that's as bad as—Jesus, help me, please, before it's too late, because I could die and then what?

"Looks like we're here," Dad says, just in time, before my heart is hardened and I don't care anymore and am totally lost. As soon as the car stops I jump out and start jabbering about how many cars are here and how cold it is and anything else I can think of to get rid of the bad words, and I breathe in as much fresh air my lungs can hold, hoping to purify my insides so I can start up the mountain a new boy.

Our plan is to hike up to Lone Pine Lake, a five-and-a-half-mile roundtrip. Dad has a large backpack filled with camera gear and our lunches, with his tripod strapped to the back of it. I'm carrying my camera around my neck and a canteen of water around my waist. I can see my breath, and I imagine I'm smoking, like Dad with his pipe, but Mom would be smoking the other way, smoking mad, if I really tried it. My fingers, even in gloves, feel numb.

The trail begins in a thick forest, and the light is so dim Dad has to shine a flashlight to keep us from tripping on rocks and branches. He says it's best to make pictures when the sun is low, so he's eager to get as far as possible before it rises.

The trail soon gets steeper—much steeper. I'm already gasping for air, not sure how I'm going to survive the rest of the day. About a half mile later we come to the first creek, small enough to hop across, but soon we come to a larger one, and there's no way we're going to jump over it. Our map says it's the North Fork of Lone Pine Creek. I'm nervous because we'll have to step from one boulder to the next. Dad says it's best not to think much about it, to just charge ahead, which is what I do, somehow making it to the other side without getting wet.

Dad is like a kid who found a lost toy. He points out every tree and bush. "That's pine—you know pines, don't you?—and see that smaller one?—manzanita—don't you love it out here, Johnny?"

He's practically skipping up the trail. For me, things turn bad. My mouth and nose never felt so small. I gulp oxygen, suck it in like I've been pulled up from the bottom of Mission Bay, and my heart is about to pound out of my chest.

"Dad, how about a rest?"

"Sure, good idea."

We sit on a large stump and check out the view. The rising sun is making an uneven pattern of light and shadows, like a weird checkerboard for giants, stretching across the Owens Valley to the Inyo Mountains.

Dad says, "Hey, look at this." He stands, holds his hand up to shade his eyes, and surveys the scene carefully. "A guy just might get something here."

As he sets up his tripod and reads the light meter, he calls the School of Basic Photography back into session.

"Remember, when shooting black and white, it's all about contrast. Anyone can snap a color picture of a mountain. The mountain itself is beautiful! You can bet there're a hundred different postcards of this very scene. But what will make it a *photograph*? Contrast, balance, different textures—all composed to grab the viewer's attention. You see what we've got here? In the foreground, trees. We want to keep them dark, but not too dark or we'll lose the detail. And out there, the bright desert? We want to keep it light, but not too light or it'll be washed out. See the challenge?"

It's more complicated than I realized.

He says, "But don't worry about that now. Just fire away and enjoy yourself."

So I take several because I figure the longer we stay here, the more I can rest. I linger over each shot, studying possibilities. Fiddling with the light meter—anything to look busy. It works for about fifteen minutes.

Up we go, up and up and up. Once again we have to cross Lone Pine Creek, this time on logs that are as slippery as snot on a doorknob. (I heard Jeff Miller say this, and he has even grosser ways of talking about slick stuff that I'd better not repeat.) Actually, falling in the water doesn't seem all that frightening anymore. If it happened we'd stop a few minutes and I'd get a breather. But we make it across and continue through a thickening forest.

Dad says, "We're almost to the lake, the highest point of our hike."

"Good. I'm starving."

He stops suddenly.

"Look—the shafts of light falling through trees. Interesting, don't you think? Let's try to capture it."

Photographs are like wild animals for him. He takes off his backpack and starts the chase.

I lost interest in photography about three hours ago.

"Come on, Buddy, see what you can do with this."

With no enthusiasm I decide to take a picture of a branch still covered in snow. Looking through my camera, I move back to get the tip of the branch in the frame. Dad says to watch the tips of things, and because of the badness in my soul I imagine him saying to watch the tits of things, and probably because I'm once more thinking about tits, I'm not paying attention to where I'm stepping and I slip on a piece of ice and fall backward, over the side of an embankment.

Everything happens so fast I don't have time to be afraid. I slide and then start rolling, and I can't stop—rolling and rolling, the world spinning and spinning—and everything is a blur. Maybe I roll only three or four times, maybe thirty or forty. You're not exactly counting when something like this happens. My whole life isn't flashing in front of me, as you might expect, considering what they say about drowning or crashing in planes. I'm mostly aware of the strap pulling at my neck and camera bouncing around my head, and I'm worried it's getting wrecked until it hits me hard—bang!—on the forehead.

The next thing I know, Dad is saying, "Johnny, Johnny!" He's kneeling over me, his face red and wet. When I move, he tells me to be still for a moment so he can make sure no bones are broken. He gently moves my arms and legs, one at a time, and deciding everything works, carefully slides his arms underneath me and lifts me to his chest and holds me tightly.

It takes an hour to crawl back to the trail. I keep telling him I'm sorry and I hope I didn't ruin my camera, and he tells me not to worry, he's just happy I'm not hurt worse than scratches on my neck and a cut on my forehead. Blood from that cut is smeared on his cheek.

We continue hiking to the lake, which turns out to be a disappointment, if you ask me, given the trouble to get here, and we have lunch—a lunch that's the best I've ever eaten. I had no idea a peanut butter sandwich and an apple could taste so good.

On the way back down, walking by the place where I fell, Dad says, "At least I got off a shot before you screamed."

Then he throws me a look over his shoulder and smiles.

Seventeen

John fingered the scar on his forehead as Pat prepared the third print. His father would have taken him to the doctor had he realized the depth of the cut. But it healed, even without stitches, and the remaining mark, half an inch above his right eyebrow, was hardly noticeable. The print, kept immersed in developer by Pat's rubber-tipped tongs, changed from muddy gray to sharply contrasting blacks and whites. It was an old building with a central door flanked by two large windows. In the left was an outline of what appeared to be a seal, the kind that swims and barks and can be trained to balance a ball on its nose. Above the door a sign read The Pelican

"That mean anything to you?" Pat asked.

"Not at all. You?"

"No. But it must have to your father."

John studied it carefully as it soaked in the stop bath and fixer, in part because he wasn't eager to give Pat the fourth negative. But when that could no longer be avoided, he said, "I'm not sure we should bother with this one."

She held it up to the safety light. "Ah yes."

"The only mystery is why he sent it to me."

"You mean besides putting your kids through college?"

"You think it's still worth something?"

"My dear, are you serious? Your father would have sold limited rights to the poster company. Not only would he have restricted the number they could make, he would have demanded they work from a print he sent them, not from the negative. Sure, thousands of illegal pictures are out there, but they're copies of copies, not the real thing. Your father probably kept a few original prints, I wouldn't know. If so, collectors would pay big money for them. Hard to imagine what they'd give for this negative."

She looked at John.

"What do you think? Should we print it?"

"If you want to."

"It feels like trespassing, but here we go . . ."

As it came to life in the developer—the beautiful face, half hidden in shadow, and the full breasts with a sand smudge on one, and the backside barely visible as a blurred curvature beyond her shoulder—Pat put her arm around John's shoulder and said, "It *is* quite a photograph, you know."

"If you say so."

They dried the prints and thanked Sammy Barnett for his darkroom. Pat couldn't resist the temptation to show what they had done.

"Wha...what?" he stammered. "You just printed that *here*?"

"Yes," she said, "which means that enlarger of yours has a whole new value." She pecked him on the cheek and added, "It's a long story, Tommy. Someday I'll tell you, if you buy the drinks."

Brewster's Mechanical had finished work on *Tuesday's Child*, but neither John nor Pat wanted to sail to San Diego that night, so they rented a slip at Oceanside Marina. After securing the boat they walked around the perimeter of the harbor to The Chart House.

The waiter wore a baggy Hawaiian shirt and spoke at length about reductions and purees and partnered flavors, but John paid no attention because he had already decided on steak. Pat agreed that sounded good. They ordered a bottle of Zinfandel, which in the light of sunset glistened in their glasses like a clear ruby.

John said, "To the bonds of friendship."

"Here, here."

They clinked harder than necessary, but the stemware withstood the hit, even as their friendship had survived the blow of neglect. John thought it strange that you can feel closer to someone you haven't seen in years than to those you see every day; some relationships, bound by chains of joy or pain, can't be broken even by years of silence. They both, in their own way, had loved Logan Stanhope and had a fissure in the heart because of his abandonment and now his death.

They stared out the window, neither saying much, using the changing light—yellow to red to violet to deep blue—as reason for reverie. In John, pictures of desert and forest and *Nude on the Beach* multiplied memories until, by some law of emotional physics, their increasing mass and velocity began blowing against the breakwater he had maintained for many years. A roiling storm was rolling toward him, but having dinner in a nice restaurant meant that for now he had to stay out of its way. So he focused on Pat: he asked about her business and her retirement, and she in turn asked about his work, his free time, and his romances. He told her about Megan, a topic that carried them through the rest of the meal.

Back in *Tuesday's Child*, John hugged Pat and went to his cabin. He fell asleep almost before he crawled in the V-berth. But he wakened to an ill-tempered wind slapping lines and whipping canvas and tilting his bed hard to the right. His watch, held up to the window, said it was almost three o'clock. He readjusted his body and told himself he would soon fall asleep, that he was dropping into peaceful unconsciousness, that it would just be a matter of minutes . . . But it was no use.

He was at Weaver's Gas and Oil, not in his dreams. Was the old man still alive? Was he still photographing that scene? Nothing there, really, just barren landscape, and yet, the longer he looked, the more he saw. That's what his father was saying, of course: keep looking, there's more. All right, point made. And a similar one from Mount Whitney: increase your depth of field. Fine, got it. But wasn't that the problem? The more he saw, the less he loved. And why send *Nude on the Beach*? Why remind him of that girl on the beach who had ruined their lives, his mother's and his?

John was now curled on his side and weeping, sobbing from a place so deep it was like throwing up, and he could feel his chest and stomach contracting as if trying to squeeze something out.

Why did you leave me? Why did you leave me with a mother who couldn't cope, who couldn't survive your unfaithfulness, who was damaged beyond repair?

And as he cried he was no longer in a V-berth but on Mount Whitney, on the side of an embankment, and he saw tears flow down his father's blood-smeared face and felt arms around him, and that embrace, he realized, was what he wanted, what he had always wanted, and the longing for it had been the black hole at the center of his being. The primal conflict spewed out, unrestrained—*I hate you and I miss you, I hate you and miss you, I hate you and miss you*—until at some point he was no longer just feeling it but saying it.

"I hate you and I miss you."

If Pat had knocked, he didn't hear it. She was sitting next to him, stroking his back. When he became aware of her, he moved closer and rested his head on her lap.

"I miss him, Pat," he sobbed. "I really miss him. But why do I miss someone I hate?"

Eighteen

B efore daylight dawned, something else did, too: John's conviction that finding his father would likely include finding part of himself. His first words to Pat that morning were "Get me back to terra firma!"

She saluted and said, "Aye, aye."

A resolute wind blew them to San Diego in good time. And it brought a storm. As they rounded Point Loma, raindrops began moistening the deck and bouncing in tiny leaps off the surface of the bay; by the time they motored into Pat's slip, the raindrops joined forces to become a deluge.

Pat said, "Stay in touch, friend."

"This time I will." And John heard himself say three words he hadn't said to another person in many years. "I love you."

"I love you, too." She cupped his face in her hands, like a mother holding her child, and kissed him on the lips.

He sprinted down the dock to the parking lot using his sweatshirt as an unsuccessful umbrella. His pants, soaked and clinging to thighs, reminded him of the misadventure at Weaver's Gas and Oil. He paused a second or two at his car, worried about its leather, but decided engineers must have concocted something to protect it. He cranked up the heater and squirmed around, trying to get warm air blowing up his legs; he even considered driving home in his underwear until he pictured getting pulled over by the CHP (always a possibility), and then what?

Into his CD player he slid the *Mass in B Minor,* his first choice if stranded on the proverbial island. Bach had poured everything into it, from human misery to divine glory, and often, when listening to it, John edged closer to believing that Something More might be at work after all. Before turning onto Harbor Drive, the deep notes and dark harmonies of the

"Kyrie eleison" reached into him and pulled out feelings that were possibly close to prayer. Lord, have mercy. John wasn't certain there was a Lord, much less One who would listen to him, but the music expressed hope that if he were about to tumble off another mountain a mercy would hold him as his father once had.

The "Gloria in excelsis Deo" seemed to soar into the sky, and like in a cheesy movie, the clouds parted and a shaft of light beamed onto the Pacific, transforming dull gray into shimmering blue-green. The "Credo in unum Deum," coming somewhere in Orange County, moved him to join tenors and basses in unison affirmation—one voice, one God, and never mind the driver in the Audi who laughed when he saw John belting it out as if he really believed it. And finally, the "Dona nobis pacem" welcomed him home, voices and trumpets swirling upward, a mellifluous supplication for the world and most of all the human heart: grant us peace.

John kicked the soggy newspapers that Joe had forgotten to retrieve into his slate entryway, dropped his bag, and immediately called Megan.

"We still on for tonight?" he asked.

"I don't know. Maybe it's not a good idea."

"Megs, listen. I know I've been confusing. A total pain. *Nole contendere.*"

"You can drop the Latin bullshit anytime."

"Fine. But would you *please* come over?"

After about five seconds of silence, which seemed to John like five hours, she said, "I'll be there in half an hour."

That gave him enough time to unpack and shower before she arrived, and when she did, she greeted him with a surprisingly warm hug.

"Have you had dinner yet?" he asked.

"Yes. I had put something in the microwave before you called. But if you're hungry, go ahead. I'll have a glass of wine."

John heated a can of clam chowder and opened a bottle of chardonnay. They talked about the weather and marked time until he finished eating. He washed the bowl and spoon, and he wiped off the countertop and realigned their empty glasses before pouring more wine. Finally he led her into the living room and sat her next to him on the couch.

"It's hard to know where to begin. Perhaps the best place would be these pictures." He had hidden them under a back issue of *The Atlantic* on the coffee table. "My father left me four negatives. I went to San Diego to visit his former partner to get help printing them."

He revealed one at a time, trying neither to ignore anything important nor bore her with details: the Mojave Desert and Mount Whitney and the mysterious Pelican.

"Looks like a bar," she said.

"That's my guess. But where? There must be twenty with that name on the California coast. I'm assuming it's in or near Mendocino."

When they came to *Nude on the Beach* she gasped, "Oh! I've seen that!"

"No doubt."

"I had no idea it was your father's."

"It's what made him famous."

"It's what made me quit sleeping on my stomach. My girlfriends and I, we *hated* this picture. Who is she, anyway?"

"I don't know her name, if that's what you're asking. Actually, I don't know much about her—except the not-so-minor fact that she caused a great deal of pain."

"How so?"

"Because of her, my father left Mom and me. As you might imagine, this picture has haunted me most of my life."

"John . . ." Megan paused, as if hesitant to complete her thought.

"What? Say it."

"Your father's leaving must have been traumatic. I understand that. But you know, it happens every day, doesn't it? The home-wrecking younger woman. I mean, it must have been difficult. I don't want to trivialize it. But it was quite a few years ago."

Her tone was gentle, but John heard her comment like an accusation.

"Why didn't I just buck up? Why am I still whimpering about a disappointment from the past?" His words came out measured and quiet, almost a whisper; but he was struggling to control a rising emotion. Was it anger? Or fear of crossing a boundary he had never approached with anyone else? Or a secret desire that had finally broken loose? He would eventually decide it was all of the above—anger, fear, longing—and something else, too, something he did not recognize at the time: love for Megan.

"John, I think you're—"

"Let me tell you the rest of the story, then. Imagine you're my mother. You're not too stable, remember, even in the best circumstances, and then your husband ditches you for another woman. That would be bad enough, agreed?" John was still speaking deliberately and softly, not looking at Megan but at their reflection in the piano opposite them. "But then, after the divorce, you see pictures of The Other Woman everywhere. Every time you turn around, there she is, staring at you, taunting you with her perfect face and breasts. And what do you do, Megan? That is, what do you do if you're my mother? I'll tell you.

"You find a rope in the garage and you make a loop at one end and you slide the loop over your head and you climb up a ladder and tie the other end around a beam in the garage and then, Megan, you jump off the ladder and you fucking kill yourself. That's what you do, if you're my mother. You kill yourself so your son can come home from college and find you hanging there with flies on your blue face."

John's hands were white, gripping his knees to steady trembling arms, and his eyes were unblinking, still staring at the piano. He had not planned to say this. He had cut through barbed wire and taken them into No Man's Land, into the place he had spent much of his life fleeing. And now he felt exposed, ashamed.

"I'm sorry," he said. "I didn't mean to—"

"Shush." She moved closer, leaning her head against his shoulder. "John, I had no idea."

"You couldn't have known. It's something I've kept hidden, even from myself most of the time. This is why my feelings about my father aren't simple. He didn't tie the knot and string her up; he didn't *murder* her. But he walked away when she was clinging precariously to the edge of sanity, and his selfishness contributed to her death.

"But—this is the weird thing, Megs—early this morning I realized how much I miss him. The famous Logan Stanhope did something unconscionable, but he was my father, the only one I had. And now, I have to follow the clues he left, see where they lead. Then . . . well, I don't know what. I suppose I'll have it out with him, one way or another."

That night John and Megan didn't have sex but they made love. He had revealed a terrible secret, yet her arm remained draped over him and her heart seemed to hold the whole of him. It was an answer, in part, to his plea: "Kyrie eleison."

The "Gloria" came early the next morning. In a semi-conscious state, John cuddled closer, and Megan, feeling his desire, covered him with her own desire, and the clouds parted and a shaft of light fell upon them. And if that also seemed an answer to prayer, it was in a way that did not wholly satisfy but intensified the longing and made him cry again, "Dona nobis pacem." Grant us more of this peace.

Nineteen

The following Saturday, John was on his way to Mendocino. Bernice had tracked down a business on Main Street called The Pelican, and a telephone call confirmed that in a window by the front door was a seal. So he packed and headed west. The most direct route would have been up Interstate 5, exchanging beauty for speed, but he knew he had to stop at a sandy cove three miles south of Carmel at Point Lobos.

John was surprised at how easily he extricated himself from responsibilities. You like to imagine you're indispensable, but step out of the pool and water smoothes over pretty quickly. It helped that others supported his quest. Megan declined the invitation to join him, despite attempts to bribe her with a weekend in Carmel, a night at the St. Francis, and wine tasting through Sonoma County. She still had a job, she said, which happened to involve an upcoming show, and besides, there are some things you have to do by yourself and this was probably one of them. Bernice saw it as an opportunity to get a new filing system in place without being pestered. Mr. Lambert not only embraced his request for a leave, he embraced him, literally.

He left early, well before daylight. Traffic on the 134 and 101 was so light he had to keep an eye on the speedometer. By Ventura the sun had turned the ocean deep green, with waves barely large enough for a lake and air so crystalline he could see the Channel Islands. Summer had scorched away all hint of green on the Sierra Madre Mountains, but even robed as friars they were a dramatic backdrop to Carpinteria, Montecito, and the palm-lined streets of Santa Barbara.

He stopped for breakfast on State Street, lingering over the *Times* and sipping coffee. He had little to do that day, having planned to stay in

Cambria, only a couple of hours up the coast. But should he press on to Carmel? Something held him back, perhaps fear of what awaited at Point Lobos.

About noon he turned onto Highway 1, a two-lane road hugging the shoreline, and started watching for the Monterey pines that appear near Cambria. He had been there before, several times, and liked it. He thought of it as from the same family as Carmel—artsy and hugging the rocky coastline—but humbler, without the pretensions of its glamorous sibling. After a sandwich from a shop in town, he browsed through a few galleries and a bookstore before registering at the Sea Otter Inn across from Moonstone Beach.

The room depressed him. It had an ocean view, a fireplace in the corner, and an excellent bed. What it didn't have was Megan. He could only hope she might have second thoughts about not accompanying him. So he called her.

She was not exactly rude, just businesslike.

"You sound distant," he said.

"John, I want to be with you." She paused a moment and then continued. "I hope this doesn't sound bitchy—can you hear the sweetness in my voice? An unfamiliar sound, I know, given the way I've been lately. What I'm trying to say is, it won't help either of us if you call with blow-by-blow descriptions of everything you're doing. If you need to talk, fair enough. But why make it harder than necessary? I miss you."

"I miss you, too."

He sat on the edge of the bed, feeling alone and sorry for himself. But he pulled out of the funk with a run along the bluffs. The wind's bracing slap and refreshing aromas, the surf's swooshing sucks and crashing climaxes, the sun's sliding down the afternoon and spangling the sea—it lifted him from the pit as if the last trump had sounded. All that had happened in his life, it seemed, for good or for ill, had led to this moment, and he was standing on the threshold of an open door. The feeling—something deeper than optimism—remained through dinner and into his room for the last half of the Dodgers' game and twenty pages of Dostoyevsky.

It was there even in the morning as he drove toward Big Sur. After two cups of questionable coffee (thanks to the small pot in his room and something called "Morningstar Blend"), he left Cambria as the eastern hills gained color and texture and depth, and the sky went from blue to turquoise to near-white. Beyond San Simeon a blanket of fog lay tucked against the chin of the Santa Lucia Mountains and covered the road ahead of him, but it finally lifted just before the hairpin turns where the road dips nearly to the water and ascends over a thousand feet, winding around precipitous headlands and into narrow canyons while wedged between calamitous drops and adamant rock. His father had loved this landscape, and John saw him once again hunched over a tripod, photographing misty coves and exploding waves and regiments of redwoods.

John stopped for breakfast at Nepenthe, the restaurant with a view as from an eagle's nest. His father and he had lounged on its deck many times during that fateful summer, having lunch and killing time between morning and evening shoots. His father would puff his pipe, gazing contentedly at the water below, or perhaps stretch out on a bench for a nap, while John would sneak downstairs to the gift shop and troll for erotic passages in the books of Big Sur's most famous literary resident, Henry Miller.

Twenty

I'm sticking to the speed limit as I drive down from Napenthe in Dad's 1974 Volvo, but Henry Miller has my imagination racing. It's near the end of the summer of '82. I'm in Carmel, assisting Dad in the darkroom and doing odd jobs for a couple of galleries. This is the second summer he took a break from portraits and rented a small apartment to be near Big Sur and Point Lobos and his artist friends. For him, going to Carmel is like a Jew going to Jerusalem. Edward Weston lived here, after all, and Ansel Adams still does. Hell, the town was founded by writers and artists, not counting Father Serra. I've been saying "hell" a lot this summer, my first regular swear word, which I suppose proves Mom's point that I shouldn't be here. She's afraid I'll be tempted by immoral influences and the artist's lifestyle, but as far as I can see that lifestyle is mostly worrying about money. To tell the truth, though, there are a few things I wouldn't want her to know: that I've been saying "hell," for example, or that twice I've been to the beach with one of Dad's pipes, or that I've been reading the nasty parts in Miller's books.

This morning Dad said he was going to be busy all day, so I could borrow the car if I wanted to. You could've knocked me over with a weak fart. The thing is, I don't have a driver's license. I'm sixteen and all and have been practicing with Dad, but haven't gotten around to taking the test. He said, "You don't have many days left here. Just be careful. And be back by dinnertime."

He didn't get an argument from me. Twenty minutes later, I cruised Ocean Avenue with my arm hanging out the window and the radio blasting, praying that Tracy would see me as I drove by. I doubted that God would get involved in something like this, especially since I was breaking the law. Still, it didn't hurt to ask.

Tracy works at Haagen-Dazs, and there's something between us. We haven't spoken about anything except ice cream, but if you could hear the way she says "Two scoops or one?" you'd know what I mean. The last time she asked I responded "Two are always better than one" and plastered a smile on my face that left no doubt about what I meant. Handing me the cone, she let my fingers wrap around her fingers long enough to feel the chocolate-caramel swirl on them, and the best part is, she winked. So that's why I cruised up and down Ocean Avenue six or seven times, driving as slowly as possible in front of her store.

Eventually, though, I headed south on Highway 1, pretending to be in a Porsche and not a gutless Volvo. I would brake just before entering the curves, and then hit it hard on the way out. Dad probably wouldn't want me to drive this far, but he didn't say I couldn't.

When I got to Nepenthe I was hungry, so I ordered French Fries, which I ate quickly in order to get downstairs to *The Tropic of Cancer*. It didn't take long to find the interesting stuff. I couldn't tell you what some of the words meant, not that I haven't heard them before. I admit I'm pretty stupid about sex. I mean, I know there are facts of life. I'm just not too clear about all of them. Dad hasn't done much more than give hints, and as for Mom, she gives the impression that any decent, God-loving person would never even *think* about such things, let alone do them. So where does a guy learn this stuff? From friends? Can you imagine being in the locker room, when everyone's bragging about doing this or that with girlfriends, and saying, "Hey, wait a minute, what's a prick?"? When they stopped laughing, they'd let you know you are one.

So I was researching the subject at Nepenthe's bookstore, and I must have been learning something because I didn't hear the saleslady walk up to me. I don't know how long she stood there, but I about had a heart attack when she said "The author lived not far from here, you know." She had long gray hair that had been braided and wound around her head, and she wore a crystal pendant and a flowery skirt that went to her ankles.

"Sorry to startle you," she said.

"I was just, ah . . ."

She patted my shoulder and said, "Don't let me interrupt."

She was being nice and all, but I decided it was time to get the hell out of there.

That's why I'm thinking about sex on the way down the hill. I like to imagine doing it. With Tracy. But I can't imagine doing everything in that book. One thing . . . yikes! Let's just say a good Christian wouldn't do *that*. Hell—maybe I should switch to heck, since I've got enough on my plate sinwise, which would mean big trouble if a car came around the bend and plowed into me—a good Christian wouldn't even *read* about it. But there I was, studying Miller's descriptions as carefully as Mom does the Bible. And as long as I'm being honest, here's maybe the worst part: I actually got hard right there in the bookstore. I'm a total scumbag.

If only I could get baptized in the Spirit. No matter how many prayers are said for me, it never takes. But I might get the victory over this sex business if I spoke in tongues. Which makes me think of the tongue, which makes me picture again what someone in the book did with his tongue. Now you know why my favorite verse is "Oh wretched man that I am! Who will separate me from this miserable body?" or words to that effect.

I need to do something wholesome to get my mind off women in general and Tracy in particular, something I can tell Dad about. So I stop at Point Lobos. This morning I threw my gear into the car to impress Dad. Now I really want to use it, to be creative rather than perverted. The parking lot is packed, not surprising in August. Eventually I find a spot, and after filling my pockets with film and attaching my camera to my tripod, I walk toward the water, breathing deeply, exhaling filth and sucking air; it's crazy, I know, but I've always had the impression that large quantities of fresh air will make me cleaner on the inside.

I've spent the summer hiking here, making sorry imitations of Weston's cypress trees and eroded rocks. This afternoon, though, I want to find somewhere new, not overrun with visitors. So I follow the South Shore Trail past The Slot and Weston Beach and on to Bird Island Trail. Near Gibson Beach I leave the trail and crawl down an embankment. I push myself between trees and through bushes, hanging on to vegetation as I slide toward a little cove that caught my eye.

The sky is dark blue, the water even darker. Waves are crashing against jagged rocks. I've learned, through plenty of screw-ups, that getting a good picture at Point Lobos is harder than you might think: you've got a straight horizon and angled surf and wind-bent trees—it's not for amateurs. Even so, I'm giving it another go. I lengthen the legs of my tripod and get it as stable as I can on the embankment.

As I'm working on a composition, I hear a woman's voice. But the beach looks empty. Did I imagine it? No, there it is again, and now laughter. How could anyone get down there? And where is she?

Now I'm curious. I leave my tripod and move toward the voice. After a few steps I see bare calves. So I edge myself along the embankment as quietly as I can and see bare thighs, and even though my footing is uncertain, I keep going because after Henry Miller and everything else, I would keep going even if I were crawling along the top of Mt. Everest, and sure enough, I see a bare bottom. I'm not kidding. And with another tiny step I see all of her, and I mean *all* of her, lying on her stomach. I kneel behind a bush, panting but doing my best to keep quiet so she doesn't hear me. I'm close, close enough to see she is wet and sand has stuck to parts of her. I shouldn't keep watching. But I can't stop, God forgive me. This is the first time I've seen a naked woman, in person anyway. She rises on her elbows, exposing her breasts, and I swear, it's a wonder I don't pass out.

I'm now touching myself. Down there. Pushing on it feels good, and without thinking, I unzip my pants and really rub it. I've never done this before, not this much anyway, but I don't even think about stopping, it's just too . . . too . . . and suddenly the thing explodes, and in that instant everything feels so wonderful and then so wet, and I realize that whatever happened is what sometimes happens in my dreams. Now I *really* hope she doesn't see me, now I suddenly feel awful, as though I've done something not just to myself but to her as well.

Wiping my hand on dirt, I hear her again. Did she see me? No, she seems to be talking to someone outside my view. She laughs again, and then I hear another person laughing, a man, and not just any man. Someone I know.

My father.

I crawl up the embankment, as fast as I can, using one hand to hold bushes and the other to zip my pants and grab my tripod. What was my father doing? Is he naked, too? Is he doing it—with the same woman I've just done whatever I've done? Back at the trail other people say "Hi!" but I can't respond. I'm sick—sick at myself, sick at my father—and I have to hide behind a tree to throw up.

Now I have wet underpants, dirty jeans, vomit on my shirt. So before getting in the car I stop at Weston Beach. I wash my face and daub my clothes, and I rub my hands together in the freezing water, again and again, almost taking the skin off, and because I still don't feel clean, I rub them in the sand, scraping the grains across the surface of my skin and finally rinse it all off again.

These hands, red and itchy, are shaking so much they can barely hold the steering wheel. I'll probably have an accident—the cherry on top of this day—since I'm not paying much attention to driving and my guardian angel has obviously taken the day off. I'm afraid to face Dad. Did he see me? What'll we say to each other?

But I get home before Dad, thank God, and I strip off my wet clothes and throw them in the washing machine. How much detergent should I use? Better too much than not enough. Then I get in the shower and let hot water rain on me.

Dad was fucking her. It's a bad word and maybe I shouldn't even think it, but what he did was worse. I know what I did is bad, too, so help me, Jesus, forgive me, Jesus, and please get me through tonight and get me home.

I lather my body, coating every inch of it with soap, and rinse it off and lather up again, until I hear Dad's voice.

"Hey, Buddy, you drowning in there? Save me a little hot water!"

"OK!"

That evening Dad is his usual self, or what I thought was his self. He grills hamburgers on our deck and at dinner asks about my day. I tell him I went to Big Sur, which is the truth, and I tell him I stopped at Pfeiffer Beach, which is a lie, but I don't care, don't pause a second to worry about it, because he's *living* a lie, and it seems right, almost my duty, to give him what he deserves. He makes no comment about me driving that far.

I'm feeling terrible. On the outside, as well as the inside. My skin is crawling, itching like hell. Especially my crotch. I must have done something by rubbing so hard.

"You all right, son? You look flush."

"Not feeling so good, I guess."

"Get up a minute, let's look at you."

We stand under the kitchen's florescent lights. Dad says, "Look at your hands and arms. You itch?"

I nod.

"Take off your shirt."

My chest and stomach aren't as red as my hands, but a rash seems to be starting there, too, in patches.

Dad says, "Oh man! That looks like poison oak. You must have gotten into it at Pfeiffer Beach. There's a bunch up there. Let's see your legs."

I drop my jeans. There isn't much on my legs. Dad points to my underpants and says, "What's it like there?" I pull the elastic top away from my stomach to peek inside. My penis is covered—like peppermint frosting on cake—and my grimace tells Dad everything he needs to know. "Oh man," he says, "that must hurt!"

"Yeah, and itches."

He chuckles. "Sorry, this isn't funny. But you must have touched poison oak with your hands and then taken a leak. Did you pee at the beach?"

"Ah, yeah."

"That's it, then. Oh, Buddy, this is horrible."

"What do I do?"

"The important thing is what *not* to do. Do not—*do not*—scratch it. You hear me? That'll make it worse."

"OK," I say, not believing it could get worse.

"You might as well get in bed, and I'll go to the drugstore. Calamine lotion might help. Tomorrow we'll call the doctor, hear what he has to say."

So I start my trip through hell, or if not hell, then purgatory. Pentecostals don't believe in purgatory, but I don't feel like a Pentecostal, lying in bed with a punished penis, feverish and sweating, and wanting more than I've wanted anything—more than I wanted Tracy to see me that morning, more than I wanted the woman on the beach to roll over so I could see the rest of her, more than I wanted the male voice not to be my father's—to scratch myself. If you've ever had poison oak, you know what I mean. It's beyond bad. I can't stand it. I squirm around on the sheets, and I give in a couple of times, actually more than a couple, and softly scratch the itch and the pain.

When Dad returns he gently spreads Calamine lotion on the rash, except my penis, which he lets me do. It seems to help. Or maybe it doesn't. I can't decide. Eventually, I must have fallen asleep, because the next thing I know, the room is dark and Dad is dozing on the chair in the corner of the room.

In the morning the doctor confirms what we already know and prescribes medicine that doesn't keep me from wanting to peel off my skin. The rash spreads to most of my body, and for the rest of the week it's like the flu, except with the worst itch you can imagine. I'm too miserable to worry about anything else, which is kind of a weird blessing.

By the time I board the plane to San Diego the rash is almost completely cleared up and I'm fine, except I feel betrayed and am disgusted and can't get out of my mind the sight of that woman and the sound of my father's laughter. Every day my anger grows and gets meaner.

Why would he do such a thing?

I can't tell you how happy I am to get home, to be back with Mom. More than ever, I feel responsible for her welfare, and I vow to protect her.

A month later I find her sitting at the kitchen table, holding a letter. She says, "He's leaving us, not coming home." In that instant my world stops turning and everything starts flying off. Nothing will be the same, ever.

It's because of the woman at the beach.

Dad tries to speak with me. He telephones, offers explanations that have nothing to do with the truth; he even invites me back to Carmel for the weekend. But I want nothing more to do with him.

Two years later, a freshman at UCLA, I'm walking down the corridor of my dorm and notice, through an open door, a poster hanging on the wall of another student's room. It's a black-and-white photograph of a woman with half of her face in dark shadow and the other half aglow in the afternoon sun.

She is beautiful.

And she is my father's lover.

Twenty-One

The beach hadn't changed much in nineteen years. John kept a wary eye on poison oak as he crawled down the embankment, considerably overgrown. He couldn't get to the exact spot where he had seen his father's lover, but close—close enough to feel a slight stab of sexual energy. It was like hearing a tune that had been on the car radio during a first kiss and experiencing again, fleetingly but unmistakably, the thrill of crossing a border into a new country. This lasted only a second or two before the recollection of all that followed.

Sliding from one bush to the next, he lowered himself to the beach without breaking his neck. A swath of sand became rockier toward the waterline. He labored through the sand to where his father must have been that fateful day and looked up. Could his father have seen him? He had never even hinted at this, but was this to save them both from embarrassment?

The day was unusually warm, and John was glad to be wearing shorts. He stripped off his sweatshirt, folded it, and left it on a rock. His sandals were likely waterproof (why else would they be called Riverwalkers?), so he wore them across stones and barnacle-encrusted shells to the water's edge where a nearly-spent wave lapped over his ankles. The water was glacial. But his feet soon numbed, and he slowly waded deeper and deeper, and he debated with himself about a full plunge. The matter was decided by a large wave that struck at chest level. He dove under the next one and the one after that, until he was beyond the breakers.

At the edge of his vision something snagged his attention. When he turned, he saw nothing. He could have sworn a dark object had been there, about ten feet away. A shark fin? Terror seized every cell and synapse in his body. Should he float, be still as possible? Or swim toward shore, flailing for dear life?

It popped up again, this time directly in front of him, about three feet away, and his relief was as absolute as it was instant: an otter. And a moment later, three more surfaced. Not having one's legs torn off can make a person giddy—giddy enough to hear otters suggest a game of Simon Says. When they floated on their backs, forepaws resting on chests, John did the same; when they dove, he followed; when they dog-paddled forward (or did dogs, in fact, otter-paddle?), he used his own forepaws like a retriever after a duck. And it occurred to him that in the laughter and splashing and gasping for air, he had been graced in an unexpected place.

But he had neither the insulation nor stamina of his playmates, so he headed back to shore, catching a wave that dumped him hard on the rocks. Standing was a rude shock. A goose-bumping breeze sent him scurrying to sand, where he spread-eagled beneath the sun. He lay on his back an hour, maybe longer, half awake and half asleep, on the margin of consciousness, even as the beach where he rested was on the margin between land and sea, an in-between place. That was precisely his location, he thought: between regret and longing, between a father-aimed anger and a father-shaped vacuum, between hating Logan Stanhope and, too late, needing Logan Stanhope—needing to ask questions, to hear explanations.

This is where it all started, the exact epicenter from which so much had evolved. And maybe, for all he knew, not just for him, but for everyone, as a slimy creature who millions of years ago crawled out of water into what became human life. And from what did it emerge? The shimmering surface of the sea held John's gaze, kept him transfixed, but its greater mysteries were submerged out of sight, hidden in darkness.

A disorderly line of pelicans glided by, each skimming its left wingtip along the crest of a wave, until an outcropping of granite broke up the flight path. Some furiously beat wings and gained altitude, continuing on their journey; others circled back and dive-bombed the water, disappearing beneath its surface to emerge with pouches jerking in all directions.

He, too, would be journeying the next day, driving up Highway 101 to the city, wending along Van Ness and Lombard and onto the Golden Gate Bridge, through Marin and Sonoma counties, and finally to Mendocino. He had never been there and had no idea what awaited him, but he sensed that, like the pelicans, he would be diving into a mystery, perhaps into the darkness he had long avoided. If so, he hoped to surface with something to show for it.

Twenty-Two

John did not let himself get distracted by wineries in Sonoma County. His mission was Mendocino, and thus he turned onto Highway 128—narrow and with curves to delight a Porsche—which took him into Anderson Valley, and thus by more vineyards and wineries. But sipping his way to the coast would take time, and he wanted to arrive before dark. So he would keep resisting temptation, yes he would, even as he saw clusters of grapes, each a globe of sugary potential that would soon be crushed into contact with yeast on its surface and then—voila!—fermentation, a miracle that for thousands of years had pleasured palates and blessed spirits, and indeed, according to the faith of his ancestors, enabled communication between humanity and the divine, a miracle that was now pleading with him to turn into driveways and into this long cultural tradition and, who knows, maybe even into a spiritual experience that would fortify him for the days ahead.

He made it as far as Navarro Vineyard and Winery, where he opened the front door just as a man carrying a case had leaned himself against it to back out, which caused the man to stumble against John's shoulder.

The man said, "Ach, sorry." The voice was deep and raspy, and the two r's motored past standard pronunciation, sounding like a card fastened against spokes of a slow-moving bicycle. Scottish? His hair was a mass of graying-black curls that had been subdued into a ponytail. Each eyebrow, large enough to conceal a small animal, traveled far enough around his forehead to need its own passport. His eyes were large and dark, the corners of which glinted in the afternoon sun. Embedded in the corner of his mouth was a half-smoked cigar, which had been there for some time, judging from the reach of saliva. He wore a kilt of some sort; it was brown leather, rubbed shiny, with enough stains and drips to please Jackson Pollock. "Wasn't paying attention," he said. "Distracted by the lovelies at the bar, don't you see?"

Two women laughed. "Hey, don't blame us!"

To them he said, "Don't forget. On Main Street, just past Kasten."

One said, "Assuming we're still upright."

And the other said, "If we see you tonight, will you tell us whether you're wearing underwear or not?"

"That's best left to the imagination, dear." He rolled his eyes at John. Outside, he discharged an ear-piercing whistle. "Burns! Come on, lad!"

A brown-and-white border collie, sniffing the hindquarters of a spaniel tied to a picnic table lifted his head and seemed undecided as to whether to have his pleasure or heed the call. The man yelled louder, and Burns sauntered toward a red pickup and jumped into its cab.

The women were getting a description of the 1997 Cabernet Sauvignon being poured into their glasses by a young man in jeans and white shirt.

"The fruit's forward," he said, "but the tannins balance it nicely."

The women chewed little crackers before swirling the wine around mouths that were likely numb from the afternoon's activities.

"That guy's a hoot," the blonde said.

"Kinda cute, for an old guy," the redhead said.

John placed himself at the bar, far enough from them not to seem too friendly but close enough not to seem rude. They smiled in a manner to suggest they wouldn't be deterred by mere distance.

"Nice day for wine tasting," the blonde said in his direction.

"Isn't every day?" the redhead said, laughing, as she took another swallow.

"Up from the Bay Area?" the blonde asked John.

"No, from Pasadena. On my way to Mendocino for a few days."

"Hey, so are we!" the redhead said, as if it were a remarkable coincidence. "Where you staying?"

"Sheila! That's none of your business."

John was grateful the bartender held up a bottle of Gewurztraminer and said, "Start with this?"

"No, thank you. I'm saving myself for reds."

"All right!" Sheila said, holding up an empty glass to toast her good fortune.

"That does it," the blonde said. "We better say goodbye." To the bartender she said, "Thanks," and to John, "Have a nice trip." She grabbed Sheila's elbow and led her toward the door.

John would have liked to visit another winery but was eager to get to Mendocino, not least because it was late and he didn't have a reservation. Beyond the town of Philo vineyards gave way to redwoods so thick he had to remove his sunglasses. Glimpses of the Navarro River came into view, and the water grew wider, eventually draining open-mouthed into the Pacific, which is how John was—open-mouthed in awe—as Highway 128 joined Highway 1 and turned northward along bluffs made all the more dramatic after a dark forest. He was through the villages of Albion and Little River almost before he knew he had entered them, and then, just beyond a bridge spanning the mouth of Big River, he saw it.

"Entering Mendocino," a sign said, and in smaller print, "Population 1100." Sitting near bluffs on the south side of a small peninsula, its buildings glowed in the light of early evening. Victorian houses, businesses with false fronts, some even with wood-planked sidewalks—it could have been the love child of a New England village and a Wyoming town. John would learn that Mendocino happened through the improbable confluence of eastern entrepreneurs and their loggers and fishers, and then artists arriving in the fifties who found cheap property and inspiration from the landscape, and then in the early seventies hippies with liberated communes and hand-painted buses, and finally, retirees able to purchase property that had risen in value with marketable charm, a charm that barely escaped being too precious by the terrible beauty of an ocean that regularly signaled its willingness to sweep the whole circus into the deep blue. John would eventually see all this, but that evening he had eyes only for a certain establishment on Main Street.

And there it was, a long block-and-a-half down Main Street: a weathered white building with a window on each side of the entrance, and in the left a seal, dark red. Above the door hung a sign, painted with blue trim and red-shaded yellow letters, that identified it as The Pelican. Across the street were bluffs and the ocean beyond.

Should he park and enter? Several heads inside were bobbing; a man and woman, beneath the seal, were laughing. His pulse quickened with indistinct apprehension.

He would wait. He needed to find a room and maybe food, although at the moment he didn't feel like eating.

The Mendocino Hotel was half a block away. No vacancies, he was told by a young woman at the registration desk. Raised eyebrows accused him: seven o'clock on a summer evening and no reservation? She sighed out a couple of places he might try.

On his way into town he had passed the Alegria Oceanfront Inn. The proprietress said it was his lucky night because a few minutes earlier she had had a cancellation. Before quoting the rate per night, she had his Visa card in her hand. The room, on the second floor of the Victorian house, was not large but had a view of the mouth of Big River, still visible in diminishing light.

After changing into jeans and a navy blazer, John walked back down Main until he spotted The Mendocino Café a block up Lansing. What caught his eye was a large peace sign painted on the side of the building. The menu in the window advertised eclectic fare.

A plate of fish tacos and three cups of coffee were necessary before he felt ready for The Pelican.

Twenty-Three

The wind off the water sharpened, and John wondered if he had packed enough warm clothes. Summer was apparently a flexible idea in these parts, as other visitors were also discovering. A family of five—all in shorts, a camera slung over Dad's shoulder and a beach bag over Mom's—huddled in front of Highlight Gallery.

The youngest was drilling his finger into the window, pointing to a large Noah's Ark surrounded by an array of animals. "There's skunks, see!"

"And see the hippos?" Dad said. "All two-by-two."

"I want one."

"We can't buy just one animal. It's a set."

"The whole set, that's what I want."

"Sorry, son. Too much. Besides, it's not a toy. Just something to look at."

"But you said I could have a souvenir."

"I know but—"

Mom came to the rescue. "Hey what about the ice cream we were looking for?"

The outcome of this diversionary tactic was drowned out by a group of smokers in front of Dick's Tavern. John continued on past the hotel and more galleries and Compass Rose Leather and The Gallery Bookstore, until, just beyond Kasten, he arrived at The Pelican.

John opened the door, and conversation poured out from the crowded room. Well-worn oriental rugs created an atmosphere of tired elegance. On the right stood an elaborately carved bar, behind which hung a mirror inset with several shelves supporting the usual bottles. Overstuffed chairs and bedraggled couches bordered the room, and tables of various sizes filled the remaining space. Customers were talking and drinking and, judging from remnants, digesting burgers and sandwiches. A battered piano was in the far left corner. Red wallpaper covered the upper halves of the walls, along with framed photos of sawmills and foundered ships, and redwood paneled the lower halves. A grid of heavy beams held up the ceiling, except in the center, where a rainbow of bright colors fell from a backlit dome of stained glass. It was a circle about fifteen feet in diameter, portraying a pelican. The tip of her beak was red, and her breast was laid bare and revealed a heart dripping rubies into the open mouths of three youngsters at her feet.

Not sure what else to do, John found a place at the bar. On his right, half sitting on a stool and half leaning on the bar, towered an African-American with dreadlocks covering his back. He was talking to a diminutive Asian-American who excitedly pointed to papers in front of him.

"No, I'm telling you, this'll be big."

"I don't get it," the black man said.

"What's not to get?"

"A flying salamander?"

"Why not?"

"Salamanders don't fly."

"Duh. Of course salamanders don't fly in biology or zoology, but what about salamanders in mythology? The ancient stories of salamanders and fire? Pictures of them from the middle ages with wings? Why else do you think they're symbols for the occult? Come on, Mr. Comparative Literature, Mr. Writer of the Great American Novel! I shouldn't have to explain this to you."

"But what's Sonoma got to do with it?"

"That's the point! It's counterintuitive, opens minds. If a salamander can fly through Sonoma, make its home in the wood-burning grill of an upscale restaurant, suddenly appearing on tables next to the haute cuisine of Chardonnay-sipping Californians, getting into all sorts of mischief but in the end saving the day through magic and a good heart—think about it a minute—anything is possible!"

"All this in a *children's* book?"

"At first, yeah. A children's book for adults, know what I mean? But that's just the beginning. My buddy in the city—the guy I was telling you about who did these drawings?—he's already at work on the logo. T-shirts, business cards—"

"Business cards?"

"A way of saying you're a person of unlimited possibilities. Then comes the movie, the musical—"

"OK, whatever. Go for it." He hoisted a nearly empty glass, a toast to shut his friend up, and said, "Here's to Sonoma Sam the Flying Salamander."

The bartender had yet to acknowledge John's presence. He was at the far end of the bar, frowning as he tried to enter something on a calculator. His white hair had barely escaped its last cutting and black horned-rimmed glasses kept sliding down his nose; he was as thin as a bottle of Absolut. John waved to get his attention.

"Save your energy," a woman seated next to him said. "Jeffrey will get to you when he gets to you. And I swear, if he thinks you're waiting for him? That you're—God forbid!—impatient? He'll stay busy with other things to show who's in charge. People have been known to die of thirst sitting here."

"So what do I do?"

"Ignore him. Pretend you're just sitting at his bar for the hell of it. He's kind of like a shy cat, I guess. Don't look him in the eyes, and he might come alongside you when he's ready."

"Unusual personality for a bartender."

"More fun about twenty years ago, for sure. Then he cleaned up—meditates daily, runs marathons, cleanses bowels. Even became a Republican. You don't want to get on his bad side because he's also a volunteer fireman. The evening you chew him out? Could be just when you have a heart attack and need mouth-to-mouth resuscitation. That's a scary thought. But if dying were the only alternative, you want to believe he'd still do it. The look on his face right now makes you wonder, doesn't it?"

"You live here, I take it."

"Since 1969. I'm Meadowlark." Long brown hair flowed over substantial shoulders and most of the way down her back; a blue kerchief crowned her head; abalone shell jewelry adorned the front of her long print dress. She was redolent of patchouli, which for some reason always made John picture Mama Cass dancing in the street.

"I'm John, from Pasadena."

"Welcome."

"Can I ask you something? What's with the seal in the window if this place is The Pelican?"

"Red Seal Ale, from up the road in Fort Bragg. Not bad." She leaned forward to speak to the African-American on the other side of John. "Hey Faulkner, meet John from Pasadena."

"Nice to meet you," Faulkner said. "Here for the weekend?"

John nodded. "A few days."

"Cool." With his thumb he motioned to his other side, as if hitchhiking. "This is Wing." Then he lowered his voice to a stage whisper, "FYI: don't be too friendly, no direct eye contact or anything, or he'll be all over you about Sonoma Sam the Flying Salamander." He held up his hand, "No, don't even ask."

"You have to be careful where you look in this place."

Meadowlark said, "And no sudden movements." Jeffrey walked past, refusing to acknowledge John. "Actually," she continued, "he's in a pretty good mood today."

Eventually Jeffrey returned and set in front of John a glass of amber liquid, neat. "Compliments of the house," he said, with a tone to imply he wasn't pleased about it. "Glenlivet, eighteen."

"Wh—"

Before John could get out the question, Jeffrey pointed to the corner. At a round table sat the man he had seen earlier coming out of Navarro Winery. His hair had escaped the ponytail and partially covered his face. He was sitting with two women, the wine tasters.

Meadowlark asked, "Friend of yours?"

"No, not really. I bumped into him a couple of hours ago. We haven't even met. You know him?"

"Peter? Sure."

"Who is he?"

Meadowlark said something John didn't hear, because at that moment the man in the corner saw John looking at him and raised his hand, which held a half-empty glass of something, and this is what his lips mouthed, or what John thought they mouthed: to Logan Stanhope. Was John imagining this? What else could he have said? To luck and strength, maybe? But then the man winked.

Twenty-Four

A day in Anderson Valley had taken a toll on the wine tasters. What remained of lipstick was smeared on the rims of white coffee cups. One had crossed her legs, and the shoeless toes of her free foot were rubbing the ear of the dog that now seemed recovered from grief over the spaniel. The other slumped over the table and held her chin in a palm, until she saw John and roused herself to sit up. "Look who the cat dragged in! Or is it drug in?" She giggled and said, "Who cares?"

The man at the table stood and extended his hand. "Peter McLeod."

"John Stanhope."

"Aye, so I gathered." He still wore the leather kilt, as well as the faded green sweatshirt with a crewneck that couldn't contain hairs curling over its ragged edge. "Have a chair," he said, pointing to an empty one. And to the women he said, "Many thanks for coming by."

The blonde said, "I think we're being dismissed."

The redhead started singing the ditty, "Every party has a pooper—"

Peter said, "Now, now, let's not ruin our visit with whining, that's what Mum used to say, God rest her soul. I'll be here tomorrow, same as usual."

Both moaned, "But we have to leave tomorrow."

"Well, then, I guess it's goodbye. Pleasure meeting you." The tone of his voice dropped into authoritative depths that ended the discussion. He remained standing until the redhead put on her shoes and each had a final swallow of coffee.

The dog readjusted himself on the floor, whimpering softly at his loss. Peter sat and leaned over him. "Ah, Burnsie, you've had a good day, have you not?"

The Scottish accent was undeniable but worn smooth by American English flowing over it. Peter sat up and looked into John's eyes. He seemed to be studying him, searching for something inside of him. The scrutiny felt uncomfortable.

John said, "Thanks for the drink."

"Your father was my best friend. Others in this room would say the same. But Logan and I—" Emotion strangled the rest of the sentence. He leaned over to address Burns again. "Will you tell John I even practiced these words? Tell him I knew he was coming, just didn't know when."

Burns cocked his head as if considering how to fulfill the request, but soon dropped it back onto his forepaws and closed his eyes.

"My father left me a picture, actually a negative, of this place."

"Aye," Peter said, as if he knew.

"What can you tell me about him?"

Peter threw his head back and laughed so suddenly John flinched. "Mercy, lad, what a question!" He pulled up the bottom of his sweatshirt to wipe his eyes. He started to say something but stopped himself. "Anyway, there'll be time enough for all that."

Then he startled John again by jumping up on his chair and hollering, "Attention, please!" He waited until the room was silent. "If you're a visitor, bear with us a moment." To John he said, "Stand up. Come on, don't be shy." When John rose, Peter continued, "Friends, do you not see something familiar? Do you not see the spittin' image of Logan Stanhope, God rest his soul? Meet his son, John Stanhope."

"No way!"

"Holy shit!"

"Welcome home!"

Half the customers immediately stood and applauded.

Faulkner was the first to reach John with arms reluctant to let go. Meadowlark was next, crushing John's face against abalone shells and saying, "My God, how'd I miss it, you right next to me?"

Then came Wing and others he hadn't met, even Jeffrey, who didn't hug but nodded his head and shook hands.

Peter jumped on the chair again and shouted, "We'll not kill the fatted calf tonight. Too many vegans here! But we'll celebrate the son's arrival, that we will. A round of drinks on me!"

The mayhem eventually subsided and conversations resumed. Two servers, with nametags that identified them as Melinda (pretty face and stout) and Patch (distracted eyes and skinny) waited on customers, ferrying drinks from Jeffrey and bringing out meals from a door behind the bar.

"Patch!" Peter said, pointing to John's empty glass. "Another for our guest."

John tried to wave him off but neither Peter nor Patch paid attention, then or later, which might account for the difficulty he had remembering details when he spoke with Megan the next day. Wine in the afternoon, too much Scotch in the evening—something had to give, and what gave was lucidity. There were pats on the back, hands gripping shoulders, confidential whispers: his father will be terribly missed, a wonderful man, practically a saint if the truth were known. And that was why he kept drinking. He would not allow himself to swim in the depths of this admiration, for one fact rose above its surface like a jagged rock: this "saint" had abandoned his mother and him.

And now, alongside the mystery of his father, was Peter McLeod. Who was he, anyway? As people rotated through chairs at their table, John watched a man who was a passing parade of sun and squalls; one moment laughter, the next tears. With no opportunity to talk for the time being, John excused himself on the grounds that he needed to get back to his room while he could still walk.

Peter followed him out of The Pelican. A man approached who in some places would be "homeless" but in Mendocino, John would learn, was "alternatively housed"; he wore a trench coat that seemed not to have been off his body in a dozen years and a hat that sported a collection of bottle caps. Behind him limped a black dog, a veteran of a hard life.

Peter gave the man a generous hug and said, "Jimmy, for the love of the Almighty, get to the Presbyterian church tomorrow. It'll be shower day. You smell like the deep end of an outhouse. Then come see me. I've got a few hours of work for you."

Jimmy flashed a big smile. "OK, man."

"And here." Peter pulled out of his wallet a bill and handed it to him.

"Thanks, man."

After he left, Peter said, "Won't see him till harvest time."

"Harvest?"

"Marijuana."

"Oh, right. Any chance we can talk more, just the two of us?"

"Aye. You'll find me here, as usual." And then to Burns, standing between them, Peter said, "See him home safely, lad." He patted Burns and
hugged John. "Goodnight, then."

Burns stayed at his side down Main, past the Presbyterian church with
its steeple lit brightly against the dark night, until they reached the inn.

John patted him and said, "Thanks, buddy. See you tomorrow."

Twenty-Five

S ometime during the night John decided to call Megan in the morning. But when morning came, with aromas from downstairs troubling his stomach and sunlight from the window afflicting his head, he wasn't in the mood. Maybe talking with her would distract from his misery. So he dialed, botching the number once before getting it right.

"You haven't forgotten me, after all."

"Megs, you didn't want a blow-by-blow report, remember?"

"That doesn't mean *no* report."

"It's hard to get it right."

"I'm pouting because I miss you. In fact, I'm still in your bed. I came over to check your plants last night, and I didn't think you'd mind. I got so worked up I could barely fall asleep."

But would she forget to hang up the towels? Would she tuck the bottom of the sheet between the mattress and box spring? Would she leave coffee grounds in the pot? He was thinking clearly enough not to mention any of this. Instead he said, "Wish I were with you."

"What would you do if you were?"

John was in no condition to respond, so told of his own difficulty falling asleep in Carmel, and by the way, Anderson Valley was a pleasant surprise, and so on until he got to The Pelican.

Megan said, "I'm missing you more than you're missing me. But you have an excuse. What's it like, anyway? The Pelican."

"Definitely not The California Club. The ceiling—that's what catches your eye. In the center is a large stained-glass pelican. It scatters a rainbow through the room."

"Tiffany style?"

"I'm not smart enough to judge. It's odd, though."

"How so?"

"The picture itself. A pelican, as I said, with youngsters at her feet—"

"And mama has a bleeding heart?"

"How'd you know?"

"I majored in Art History, don't forget. Legend has it the mother will peck out her own heart if her young are starving."

"Ouch. That's going the distance."

"A symbol of sacrificial love. You see it in medieval art, the windows of European cathedrals."

"This is a long way from Europe. But speaking of love, the town seems to have had a surprising amount for my father." John told her about Peter McLeod and how people carried on about his father. He must have talked for a while because Megan interrupted with a gasp.

"Oops, sorry, John. I just noticed the clock. I've got to shower or I'll be late for work."

Limiting himself to coffee and yogurt, to the surprise of a server who repeatedly asked if he really wanted to pass on blueberry crepes, John dug running shoes out of the bottom of his suitcase and headed toward the bluffs. A trail, barely wide enough to run on, traced the edge of cliffs, sometimes not more than a foot from a precipitous drop to waves that detonated into blizzards of foam and rivered down rocks. The gray above was breaking apart, and the spreading blue mirrored itself below. He kept running, his head clearing with each mile, until the trail disappeared in a grove of cypress.

The nearest road soon ended at Lansing, forcing a turn. John chose right, assuming it would lead back to Main. It took him past a Catholic church and cemetery, dropping down a short but steep hill that leveled in front of Mendosa's Market, by which sat Jimmy, who waved and smiled. John pointed to his shorts as an apology for no wallet. He continued past Patterson's Pub and the Masonic Lodge, now a bank with an odd circle of figures atop its tower, and finally back to Main. The exercise felt so good John did one more lap.

After showering and shaving John explored the town, spending time in the bookstore where he thumbed through books filled with pictures from the past (busy sawmills and working immigrants and cavorting hippies) and paintings by local artists (Bill Zacha and Olaf Palm and E. John

Robinson) and clips from locally-filmed movies (*East of Eden* and *Johnny Belinda* and *Murder She Wrote*).

The place was beautiful and quirky, to be sure, but why had his father drawn him here? Did it reveal anything about Logan Stanhope?

John returned to The Pelican that evening, loaded with questions for Peter McLeod. The kilt had been exchanged for faded jeans, and the sweat-shirt for a fisherman-knit sweater with patches on the elbows.

Peter said, "I see you've survived a day here."

"Yes, indeed."

As soon as John sat, a warm head rested on his thigh. He petted the forehead and scratched behind ears and then stopped, assuming he had discharged his duties. But Burns was not finished. He pushed a wet nose under John's arm, demanding more. So the petting and scratching contin-ued as John ordered red wine.

When the wine came, John said to the dog, "You're a fine fellow but you'd keep me stroking your head all evening. So we have a problem. I need my right hand now."

Burns made it clear this was John's problem, not his.

John said to Peter, "Strong-willed dog."

"Aye."

An old lady with a cane came to the rescue. "Burnsie, my boy!" she said. At once the dog crawled out from under the table to greet her.

"Louise!" Peter said, as he jumped up and kissed her on the cheek. "Where've you been?"

"Visiting kids in the Bay Area."

"John, meet Louise Nygren, ninety-two years young, renowned artist, the Queen of Mendocino."

"Don't believe all that, except the ninety-two part."

"And this is John Stanhope."

"That's plain to see."

John stood and shook her hand, as Peter pulled out a chair.

"Glass of wine?" Peter asked.

"Heavens, no! After a weekend with my family, how about a mar-tini?" She situated the cane between her legs, and then examined John. "So. Cheekbones slightly higher. Same hair, almost the same eyes. I liked your dad a great deal. We had disagreements, sometimes even arguments. I wanted him to exhibit more, get out of that cave of his. About the only place you can see his work is my living room. I kept buying it, hoping it would encourage him."

"His photographs aren't in galleries?" John asked.

"Only a couple at Zacha's. He kept them to himself. You'd see him all the time taking pictures at Portuguese Cove—right, Peter? Other places, too. It frustrated me. I'd say, 'Dammit, Logan, get a show together while I'm still alive to see it.'"

"John, not that long ago, Louise and your father and I were sitting at this very table, and what did he say but 'Louise, what would you think about posing for me? It's been years since I've worked with a live model.' And Louise says, 'Nude, I assume.'"

"Peter, you'll give John the wrong idea about me. I was joking."

"And your father says, 'Absolutely. Maybe it'll be a series—The Beauty of Age. I could even include Peter, though he'd probably break my lens. Besides, I posed for you several years ago.'"

"Yes, he did. One of the best nudes I ever painted. Won a prize at the Art Center. But you know, I think he actually wanted to photograph me. I suppose he imagined interesting patterns in my wrinkles, like cracks in the desert, and a nice contrast provided by my black age spots."

John felt it was time for another glass of wine.

Twenty-Six

L ouise hoisted herself on the cane and bid all a good evening. Her place
was soon taken by others: Wing took flight with Sonoma Sam until
Peter grounded him; Starbryte distributed flyers about an upcoming ce-
ramics and jewelry show at Oddfellows Hall; James, who handcrafted gui-
tars for "aging rockers and rich suckers," wanted to meet Logan's son; and
Madison asked for Peter's signature on a petition to outlaw pony rides in
Mendocino County.

After she left John said, "Is she serious?"

"As serious as a Glasgow football game. Pony rides—think about it!—
are based on domination, and thus fundamentally related to imperialism,
which everyone knows is the result of racism, and thus ultimately a matter
of justice." Peter winked and sighed. "Ach, don't we miss our youth? The
thrill of protest! Taking over Telegraph Avenue, or barricading trustees in
administration buildings! There's nothing so energizing as righteous cer-
tainty. But I'm in no position to mock. I did my share with petitions and
placards."

"In Scotland?"

"Edinburgh University, then Princeton Theological Seminary."

"Seminary? You studied to become a minister?"

"Aye. Did, too, till I got defrocked."

John wasn't sure he heard him correctly, the way he rolled the r in
defrocked and spat out the second syllable as if he were clearing his throat.
"Did you say defrocked?"

"Not for the usual reason, sad to say."

"What happened? If you don't mind my asking."

"After seminary a congregation called me to be their pastor. Those were tumultuous times—civil rights, Vietnam, and we hadn't even started worrying about pony rides! I had more passion than wisdom, granted. But somewhere along the line Jesus of Nazareth got under my skin. I had the crazy notion that Christianity had something to do with him. That creates a wee problem, however. Actually following his teaching can get you in trouble. I couldn't believe Jesus would be happy about napalming children. Just a hunch, you know? And I wanted the church, *my* church, to take a stand. Which would've been fine, no problem. As long as it didn't cost much. But if it involved money? Well, we wouldn't want to be fanatics, would we?

"To protest the war, a big rally of clergy was planned for Washington DC. Protestants, Catholics, Jews—all sorts would be there. I had to go. That was that. So I asked the elders for money to buy an airline ticket, that's all. They said no. They were supportive in spirit (that's how they put it), but the funds weren't available because the sanctuary windows needed caulking.

"The funds seemed available to me, sitting right there in the church's bank account. I didn't exactly steal the money. I considered it an undocumented loan."

"So you went anyway?"

"Aye. Marched on the Capitol Building, we did, and had a sit-in. Wouldn't budge till the police arrested us. Have you ever been in jail, John?"

"No. That's something I try to avoid."

"Good strategy. But let me tell you, if you ever find yourself there, you want to be with people like Bill Coffin and Eugene Blake and Rabbi Heschel." He paused and then, in reverent tones, continued. "Abraham Joshua Heschel. He looked like an Old Testament prophet. As they herded us in and out of police wagons and escorted us to cells, he put an arm around me. That's all, just a gesture of encouragement."

Peter's eyes filled with tears, and he had to stop for a moment.

"These days, I cry at anything. Advertisements on TV are the worst. Anyway—where was I? So the rabbi puts his arm around me, doesn't say a word, and—I can't explain this—it feels like my real ordination, more than when the presbytery laid hands on me. That's why, when the elders fired me, I refused to leave. So the presbytery had a big trial and said it wasn't about the war but about my disregard for ecclesiastical process and defrocked me. Sorry. That's more than you wanted to hear!"

"Not at all. You don't have a congregation now, I take it?"

"No, no."

"What kind of work do you do?"

"I sit here, try to be helpful. Do odds and ends."

"I'm not sure how to ask this, but I mean, with what happened—ordained by a Jew, kicked out of the church—you still a Christian?"

"Hard to say."

The noise at the bar had been getting louder. Two women had come in wearing t-shirts. One shirt said, "If you don't like the way I drive, get off the sidewalk," and the other said, "Return Florida to Spain." In addition, a man had staggered in who appeared to have visited other bars on the way.

The man said, "What the fuck's that 'sposed to mean? Return Florida to Spain?"

"Remember Bush v. Gore?"

"More liberal shit, huh? Some of us bled for this country, and we're not gonna let you people ruin it." Now he was yelling, and he pushed his considerable gut against her shoulder in a threatening way. "You hear me? All you lesbos need is a man to—"

Before he could finish the sentence, Peter threw his right arm around the man's neck and smashed his face onto the bar. Burns followed as backup, eager to get in the fight. Peter was big and knew his way around a scuffle, but the drunk was bigger. The room had been stunned into silence; everyone quickly scattered to give them space. Jeffrey alone carried on as though nothing unusual was happening, calculating a bill at the computer. The man flailed his arms wildly, but Peter tightened his hold until he quit moving.

Then Peter leaned over close to his ear and spoke softly, almost tenderly, "I have something very important to tell you. Are you listening?" The man didn't reply, so Peter lifted the man's head slightly and once again dropped it onto the bar. "As I was asking, are you listening?"

The man grunted.

"I'll take that as a yes. God loves you. Never ever forget that. OK?"

No sound came from the man. So Peter lifted the head again and brought it down, harder this time. Peter had the advantage, twisting the man's neck and choking off his air.

"Let's try it again, shall we?" Peter said. "God loves you. Never ever forget that. OK?" The man grunted assent. "But you know what? The rest of us think you're an asshole. So I want you out of here till you sober up. And I want you to leave with the manners your mama taught you, because, trust me, you don't want to be here if I get upset."

Peter slowly released him. The man straightened up, started to say something but apparently thought better of it, and turned to leave. Burns escorted him out the door, barking a few times for good measure.

Scattered applause broke out and someone shouted, "Yo Peter! Way to kick ass!"

Peter walked back to the table, sat down, and looked at me. "That question you asked a few minutes ago?"

"What question?"

"The one about being a Christian? I don't think Jesus would've handled the situation like that, do you?"

Twenty-Seven

"So what have you learned about the great Logan Stanhope?" Megan asked later that evening.

"Not much."

"You've been gone four days. You'll have at least another day getting home. What's the plan?"

"Not sure. A few minutes ago, as I was leaving The Pelican, Peter invited me to go with him to Anderson Valley. He said it would be an opportunity to talk without interruptions."

"That's better than getting in another bar fight."

"I wasn't in it. Peter had it under control. You should see this guy."

"I'm ready to see you."

"I know. But a little more time with Peter might be important."

The next day, after a run along the bluffs and a search for his father's pictures at Zacha's Gallery (sold out), John had lunch on the deck of Bay View Café. Spread below and beyond were Main Street, the mouth of Big River, and the Pacific Ocean. The day was ardently blue, the horizon line as sharp as a knife.

John met Peter at two o'clock in front of The Pelican. He was standing next to an old red pickup; Burns was waiting in the cab.

Peter said, "Grand day!"

"Sure is. Where'd you say we're going?"

"Burning Oak Vineyards, to pick up an order." An unlit, half-smoked cigar sat in the corner of his mouth.

They turned south on Highway 1, heading through Little River and Albion and, merging with Highway 128, into Anderson Valley. Burns sat between them, an alert co-pilot.

"By the way," Peter said, "I should have mentioned we're in Mendocino County, not L.A. A truck, not a courtroom."

"Actually, I know that."

"Your jeans are fine, although being so clean they're a little dressy. But a starched white shirt?"

"Hope I don't embarrass you."

"It's Burns I'm worried about. He's very sensitive."

"What about you? How many guys around here wear a skirt?"

Peter laughed heartily, pounding his hand on the steering wheel. "Right you are, lad, right you are. But you know why they call this a kilt, don't you?"

"No, why?"

"Because the last guy who called it a skirt got—"

"Kilt. I'll be more careful. Peter, how did you know I spent time in the courtroom? I didn't say I was a lawyer."

"Don't blame you. But your father never stopped telling me."

"Really?"

"Went on and on about you, he did. When in a mood. But those times were rare. He'd withdraw, as if hibernating."

"How long did he know about the cancer?"

"About six months. A mole on his neck got weird, so a local doc sent him to UCSF Medical Center. Tests came back positive, which of course means negative. Stage IV melanoma. Then chemo—ach, that's vile. He lost weight, hair, energy, you name it—death on the installment plan."

Peter's cheeks were wet, and he fished in his pocket for a handkerchief. John said, "I suppose I'd withdraw, too, if facing death."

"He wasn't running from the future, John. He was running from the past. It wasn't the death he was facing but the death he was remembering."

"He wasn't the only one with painful memories. He made choices, some that sent my mother over the edge. Did he mention that? Did he mention that taking up with a beautiful young woman caused his wife to hang herself? Did he mention that his son had to find his own mother hanging from a beam in the garage?"

"Aye." He said this very softly, tears now flowing down his cheeks, dripping off his chin. At the next pullover he stopped the car. He said to

Burns, "Down, lad," and made him lie on the seat so he could look directly at John. "And your mother's death wasn't the only one that haunted him. When he returned from Vietnam, he carried on as best he could, tried to be a good husband and father. Loved you dearly, dearly—"

"He had a strange way of showing it."

"Did he, you think?"

"What do *you* think? Leaving a sixteen-year-old with an unstable mother, abandoning him in adolescence when he most needed guidance. Peter, we hadn't talked in almost twenty years when I heard about his death!"

"And whose fault would that be?" Peter's eyes held John's in an unyielding grip until John turned away in silence. The words had opened a crack on the hard-packed surface of John's consciousness, and he was suddenly running like the roadrunner in the old cartoons, spinning his legs to stay ahead of a widening fissure that could swallow him whole. Peter repeated himself, this time in a whisper, "And whose fault would that be?"

"I was sixteen—"

"And then seventeen and eighteen. And what of the letters, the telephone calls, the attempts to meet with you? You, too, made choices, John, and maybe for good reasons. But you know, we all edit the memoirs we're writing in our minds, and we usually delete big hunks to make more sense. Probably can't be helped. But I hope you'll remember that your father tried to stay in touch. How many times did he tell me about phone calls abruptly ended? How many times did he throw down another returned letter on a table? Eventually, he just gave up. The hand that keeps getting slapped might be slow to learn but eventually quits reaching out. You had a right to build your own life. I'm not judging the one you built, John. Just don't be questioning his love for you."

John could not acknowledge the truth in what Peter said, not at that moment, not sitting in a pickup with bees flying through open windows and Burns barking at something in a dream. That would have to happen as conversations and events from the past moved in his memory and gave it a new shape.

"We got sidetracked, didn't we? What was I saying?"

"Vietnam. When he came back—"

"Aye. Carried on as if everything was fine. Just fine. But things can be smashed to smithereens on the inside for quite a while before they show up on the outside. I tried to get him to talk about it. We'd get fat cigars and walk a mile or so in Van Damme Park until we found a big redwood to lean against, and we'd blather on and on, and occasionally real things would seep out, and sometimes, painful things. He never went into details, mind you. That wasn't his way. But after years of this, I began to understand more. Through his viewfinder he looked at smoldering villages, severed limbs, women alive but wishing they weren't, charred bodies of children. The very heart of evil. And what did he do with this, John? Think about it. He was an artist, the poor man. He couldn't just snap a picture, could he? He had to frame it and compose it, work with viewpoint and proportion and contrast. He was making art. Art! Sometimes he'd convince himself he was simply helping people see more clearly. But in a deep place he couldn't escape, it felt like spraying perfume on a pile of shit. Photography, the thing he loved, had become a tool of denial.

"There would be no going back to life as usual. Maybe for a while, not forever. If he'd been a soldier they'd have a name for it—post-traumatic stress disorder—and he'd get his VA benefits. But a lowly freelancer? All he had were his own resources. And what would that be? His art, the thing that created the stress in the first place. So he took pictures of school kiddies, aye. But at some point, maybe with a squirming third-grader, he'd look through the viewfinder and see a girl who he imagined would soon be diagnosed with leukemia, or who would get her full three score and ten but would bury her own child or get a divorce—he saw, in other words, the death underneath it all."

"So he ran? Ran from wife, ran from son, ran from responsibilities? I'm sorry for what he experienced, but does it excuse what he did?"

"No, dammit! If he'd been a stronger man, a better husband and father, he might have handled it differently. But all he had to work with was himself, a flawed human being. No, John, it's not about excusing. It's about seeing—if not the whole picture, then more of it. Isn't that why you came up here?"

John's silence answered his question.

Peter continued. "I suppose you could say he ran. Don't we all? Most of us are unaware of it, but we're doing it all the same." He took the stub out of his mouth and used it to point to his stomach. "Down here, we're full of fear and have to cope. We impose order to contain the chaos; we make beauty to cover the ugliness. You with the law, Louise with her paintings, me with my thin gruel of religion. Doesn't mean these things aren't good and true. But let's not kid ourselves. We have to manage, one way or another. Even last night's poor fool who'll be having a sore neck today."

"But we don't all abandon responsibilities."

"You're right, John. So go ahead, hate your father the rest your life if you think it'll help. But leaving your mother was more complicated than it might appear."

"What's complicated about preferring a beautiful young woman?"

Peter hesitated, but finally said, "That part of the story is not mine to tell."

He put the pickup in gear and drove down the highway to a long driveway just beyond Philo. At the end stood a small grove of oak trees, in the middle of which was a rustic tasting room. Peter suggested trying the reds while he found the estate manager and got his cases of wine.

Back in the pickup, Peter said, "So?"

"The Cabernet is worthy."

"Good. It's our house wine, which I first tasted, by the way, with your father. Actually, this is where we met. Your father was on assignment. The winery had an idea for a new label—an oak tree glowing in a sunset. Problem was, it's hard to predict sunsets. I don't know how many trips he made out here. Eventually he got one he liked, and they used it a few years.

"I was loading cases in my old pickup—believe it or not, this is my new one—and I heard a voice say, 'You'd think a man in a cloud of smoke could lend a guy a match.' With those words he fired up more than his pipe."

"So that's how Dad made his living here? Photography?"

"For a while. But it was tough."

Peter drove out to the highway and turned toward Mendocino before continuing.

"He lost energy for pleasing customers, promoting himself, taking pictures of puppies for Christmas cards. So he quit doing it, except on his own terms. He had this place at the Cove—we should put up a sign, 'In Memory of Logan Stanhope.' Any time of day you'd see him there, leaning over a tripod."

"But didn't he sell the landscapes?"

"He had a couple of galleries—one in Carmel, another in Santa Fe— that pestered him for prints, and once in a while, when strapped for cash, he'd send them something. For the most part, though, he pieced together a living from jobs around town. He worked at The Pelican a few years, tending bar, and then at Mendosa's."

"The grocery store?"

"Honorable work."

"Yes, but . . . I wouldn't have imagined him doing that. Didn't he get royalties on—"

"The famous poster? None at all. He sold the right to use the image for a one-time fee. The way things turned out, he regretted the decision. He kept the negative, of course, which is now yours, and he could have made prints from it and probably made a killing, the way Adams has with *Moonrise*. But for private reasons he chose not to do that."

Peter's emphasis on *private* signaled an end to that part of the conversation. Actually, it was the end of what was spoken until they reached the village. As the pickup lurched back and forth on the curvy road, John's mind careened among the things Peter had told him.

Twenty-Eight

After John helped Peter move the cases into a storage room, they walked through the kitchen and around a man standing next to the stove. Peter introduced him as Howie Fry, whether as joke or odd fact John couldn't tell. He was short and appeared to have sampled most of what he cooked; his remaining hair had grown long enough to be pulled into a bun and wrapped in a net. The front of his apron displayed remnants of his work.

Peter asked him, "What's cooking?"

"Usual stuff, Boss." It hadn't occurred to John that Peter might be more than an errand runner. "And tonight's special is pork belly."

Peter said, "Tell me that's not true."

"Yep. The fat on a pig's belly breaded and deep fried in more fat. Eat it fast before it coagulates! But *so* good."

"So good we'll get sued by victims, or their surviving families."

Every table was full. Melinda and Patch were running in every direction, both with stray hairs stuck to sweaty foreheads. Faulkner and Wing were already at Peter's table.

Wing said, "Where you been?"

Peter ignored the question.

Wing ignored this ignoring and launched into his current problem. "So, I need your help with Faulkner. He's being unreasonable, more than usual. You know I'm working on a children's book—"

"Oh really?" Peter said.

"Yeah, Sonoma Sam the Flying Salamander, remember?"

"Sounds interesting," Peter said as he winked at Faulkner.

Faulkner shook his head. "Don't encourage him." And to Wing, "Can't you see he's teasing you? Of course he's heard about Sonoma Sam. We're all sick of Sonoma Sam."

Wing said, "See what I'm dealing with?"

Peter said, "Friends can be tough critics."

"But friends should be willing to help, shouldn't they? I'm not asking much. All I need is for Faulkner to ask his agent to look at my book."

Faulkner said, "Man, it doesn't work that way. You know how long it took me to find an agent who would read more than my proposal? And now it's been over three months since I sent her the manuscript, and for all I know, it's fallen into a black hole, never to be seen again. I don't even know if I have an agent. And you think I'm going to muddy the water with your stupid salamander?"

Peter said, "Salamanders thrive in muddy waters."

During this exchange a large man with unkempt white hair entered The Pelican. He seemed headed toward Peter's table but stopped to shake hands, pat shoulders, and tousle hair.

Peter jumped up and said, "Saints be praised, if it isn't Father Stu back from Rome!"

Father Stu embraced him and said, "How's my favorite sinner?"

"Couldn't be better. How's the pope? You remember to greet him for me?"

"I did, but for some reason he couldn't remember you."

"And him infallible and all! Stu, meet Logan's son, John."

The priest gripped John's hand. "I heard you arrived, and I've been looking forward to meeting you, even if you hang out with these characters." He dragged an empty chair from a nearby table and squeezed it between John and Faulkner. "Your father's passing has been hard, for all of us."

Patch returned with a drink for Father Stu. "We're out of Maker's Mark. How about Gentleman Jack?"

"Fine, thank you. You've got a great staff here, Peter. Especially now that you got rid of Vern."

"Vern not working out?"

"John, what would you think of a friend who says, 'I've got the custodian you've been needing. He's doing odd jobs for me, working pretty well but needs something permanent. You should give him a try.' So because Peter here recommends him, I do just that. I hire Vern. Not much cleaning the first couple of weeks, but I think to myself, he needs to settle in, get used to the place. Today I go looking for him, search everywhere. Nowhere to be found. Finally, I decide to sweep the sanctuary myself, so I go to the broom closet and what do I see? There he is, sitting on a stool, watching a soap opera on a little TV!"

Peter said, "Everything happens for a reason, Stu. God is probably testing you."

"Let me finish. Even God couldn't have foreseen what comes next. About two hours later I'm in my office, working on Sunday's homily, and there's a knock at my door. It's Marion Burnside. She says, 'Father, I think you should see something.' She motions for me to follow, which I do, and she takes me to the women's restroom and says, 'Don't worry, no one's in here.' When we get inside, she opens the door to one of the stalls. Above the toilet is a big sign, made with butcher paper and red crayon and a squadron of exclamation points. It says, 'Ladies!!! Flush the Toilet!!! Remember, God is Watching!!!' Marion says, 'It had to be Vern.'

"Now, I ask you, John, what would you do? I see no choice but to tell Vern, 'This really isn't working out, you being the church custodian. You seem not to have the necessary skill set for this position.' I learned to talk like this at a management workshop sponsored by the diocese. *Skill set.* Anyway, as evidence I mention the sign, and he says, 'What's wrong with that?' And I say, 'Vern, everyone knows God doesn't watch ladies going to the bathroom.' He thinks for a moment and then says, 'Well, I'll make a deal with you. I keep my job, and I won't tell anyone you were in the women's restroom with Marion Burnside.'"

Everyone laughed, Peter so hard he dropped his head on the table.

A loud scream silenced the whole room.

Meadowlark yelled, "It's Jeffrey! Something's happened!"

Jeffrey had collapsed and was spread-eagle behind the bar, apparently unconscious. Peter felt his neck for a pulse and leaned close to his mouth. "Call 911" he said, as he began pumping Jeffrey's chest. Father Stu knelt on the other side of Jeffrey and made the sign of the cross on his forehead. No one even whispered. The next few minutes lasted hours, until a man and woman wearing Mendocino Fire Department jackets and carrying emergency equipment arrived and took over.

As they carried out Jeffrey on a stretcher Peter said, "I'm going with them. Faulkner, you take over. And John'll be your assistant. I'll call from the hospital when I know something."

No one was sure what to say or do. But Father Stu had the skill set for leadership. He said, "I could use another drink."

Faulkner said to John, "We're in charge. Here, take this bottle and see how many glasses you can fill."

And that's how John Stanhope, Attorney-at-Law, began his career as Assistant Bartender.

Twenty-Nine

Peter stayed with Jeffrey for the next two weeks. According to the doctor, the heart attack had been a major one; according to Meadowlark, the likely cause had been clean living. In the meantime, where decisions get made through the accumulated weight of circumstances, Faulkner and John became *de facto* managers of The Pelican. John needed training with drinks, but he left most of the pouring to Faulkner while he directed traffic and cleaned up. John found sopping and scrubbing and sweeping oddly fulfilling. He loved closing time, after the last person had left and they had readied the place for the next day, and there was a sense of completion, of work done, the feeling he had when all sides finally signed a contract, the feeling he imagined surgeons have after the last stitch is sewn.

Faulkner knew what he was doing. He had worked there several years before Peter and John's father pestered him to finish his degree in Comparative Literature at Sonoma State. His real name was Charles Wilson; he had been nicknamed "Faulkner" when an obscure journal published one of his stories. He was now working on a novel and supporting himself with any work he could find.

What about John's own work, his employment with a law firm in Los Angeles? That was the question Megan and Bernice had for him.

He had been gone almost two weeks before Bernice called. "Is this John Stanhope, the man who had a promising career as an attorney?"

"I'm your man. Remember that song?" He sang the line a couple of times. "Leonard Cohen, I think."

"You're in quite the mood. Sampling the local crop?"

"Nope. Chaste lungs, not counting the time I was walking along Main Street and a guy in front of me exhaled a cloud I couldn't avoid."

"Then it must be the seagulls and hippies."

"We're getting along."

"I thought I'd better remind you of something. Remember email? That way we have of communicating these days? My rough estimate is that you have 2,343 messages in your inbox. Didn't I tell you take your laptop?"

"Yes, well, I should have warned you about reception here. Mendocino isn't exactly high-tech. It's not that the people are backward, don't get me wrong. Most have heard about computers. But the view seems to be, if you want that sort of thing, stay wherever you came from. If everyone used email, what would happen to paper mail? And without paper mail, what would happen to the Post Office? And without the Post Office, how would you organize your day and get caught up on gossip?"

"How charming. But what should I do with your clients—your clients, by the way, who supply you with a handsome salary and the need to employ me?"

"Send out a blanket response saying I'm away from the office, and make it sound like I'm on important business. And speaking of business, what's been happening? Things falling apart without me?"

"Not that I've noticed. I passed a couple of items to your esteemed colleagues. But you should know that yesterday Owen Lambert—you might remember him, the founder of the firm?—stopped by to ask about you. I told him how wise he was to encourage you to go up there, and that you were making life-changing discoveries, on and on, even though I had no idea what I was talking about."

"You're good at that."

"Listen, just between you and me, are you coming home before Christmas?"

If John's delay perplexed Bernice, it annoyed—even angered—Megan. John called every day, relaying experiences and asking questions. But her comments had sharpened: "Are you really learning that much more about your father?" and "Too bad everyone can't take off" and "I'd find it hard to be away from you this long, but I guess we're different." John said he missed her (true), he couldn't wait to hold her (very true), and he was looking forward to getting home (actually, not so much).

Explaining why he was still in Mendocino wasn't easy. He had fallen into a comfortable routine—reading and running in the morning, lunch at the Bay View or Mendocino Café, then showing up at The Pelican and working as conscientiously as on any legal case.

Megan said, "Don't be upset, but I need to ask something. Have you met someone else?"

"Why would you even wonder?"

"You're just so predictable, so orderly. But now, it's like you're in a midlife crisis or something, and you already have a sports car."

"Megs, trust me. I haven't found another woman. I think about you all the time and I can't wait to see you again. But to be honest, I have met others—the regulars at The Pelican."

He would not have chosen to be with these people, nor would they have chosen him. Too little in common, too different. Yet there they were, thrown together, and somehow he felt larger just getting through each evening. Maybe, he thought, necessity has gifts unknown to freedom; maybe there's value in having to get along with people you're stuck with. He had been part of groups before, but this might be the first time he had been part of a community.

"Megs, listen. I have an idea. Come up here, visit me. Next weekend or the one after that."

"Or the one after that! How much longer are you staying? You sound like a prisoner who might get visiting privileges. Why don't you come see me? Just a short visit, nothing taxing. Maybe even see if you still have a job, you know?"

John missed Megan and Bernice, his townhouse and his income. But he sensed he wasn't finished in Mendocino. There was that comment from Peter: "That part of the story is not mine to tell." John would have asked about it by now, but Peter wasn't around much, and when he was, he flew through like a pelican skimming the crest of a wave, close but never touching. So he couldn't leave, not yet.

Whose story could it be?

Only one person's.

Jeffrey's homecoming was a surprise. The Pelican was packed; besides more tourists than usual, it was hosting the monthly meeting of the History Book Club. Judging from the noise in the corner, the gathering was more about drinking than reading. But they explained to John that a discussion of David McCullough's *Truman* had to include bourbon, given the president's fondness for it. It was actually their duty to imbibe. John was setting down the last glass when Peter and Jeffrey walked in the front door. Jeffrey was leaning on Peter with one arm, and with the other he waved to applauding locals.

The gaiety of the moment caused John to do something that surprised everyone, including him: he set his tray on top of the old piano, lifted its dusty key cover, and started banging out "For He's a Jolly Good Fellow." The piano was out of tune, like most of the singing. When they finished there were shouts of "More!" But what could he play? A Bach fugue was hardly appropriate. He frantically scanned the music in his memory and found one he had learned for a fraternity reunion. Without sitting, to remain authentic, he hit the top key and glissaded all the way down, breaking into his best rendition of Jerry Lee Lewis's "Great Balls of Fire!"

The whistles and applause were excessive, so he responded with an excessive bow before heading back to the bar, but before he could get there, someone thrust out a leg to block him. The shouts grew louder. He threw a desperate glance to Peter, who smiled and gestured to keep going. But with what? His non-classical file seemed empty, a total vacuum—except the music imprinted on his DNA, the old gospel songs of his boyhood. Surely this wouldn't be the time or place, would it? A southern/rock style might help. Because he couldn't think of anything else, he started with "Just A Closer Walk With Thee" and went seamlessly into "What A Friend We Have In Jesus" and finally, changing tone, into "Amazing Grace." He was too embarrassed by the songs even to look up, but when he finally did, he saw customers holding drinks aloft, as if waving candles in a stadium, and some, he could have sworn, with eyes closed.

When he stopped, there was silence. Then Peter's voice boomed out. "He'll be here tomorrow night, too! Right, John? About nine o'clock?"

John held out both hands, palms up, as if helpless before the acclaim. He made his way over to Peter and said, "The least you can do is set out a jar for tips. And get the thing tuned before tomorrow night!"

Thirty

Jeffrey stayed long enough to receive good wishes before Meadowlark took him home. After hugging him goodbye, Peter sat in his usual chair and Burns lay at his feet.

"John," he said, "I'm grateful for your help around here. I didn't mean to take advantage of you, I hope you know that. But Jeffrey has no other family." As he moved his head and shifted in his chair, a patch of red light from the stained glass above bounced around his face and chest.

"I'm glad I could help. But now we need to talk."

"Aye."

"I've enjoyed being here—showing up every afternoon, meeting interesting people, getting to know the regulars, even sponging the bar and sweeping the floor."

"Not your usual activities, I would guess."

"No. And I've gained insight about my father. You and others here must have been a family for him."

"I hoped you might experience some of this. I confess, that's why I didn't feel any urgency to hurry back."

"Before I go, however, I'd like a few more answers."

"What are the questions?"

"Well, for example, when we went to the winery, I said something about him leaving Mom for a beautiful young woman, and you said, 'That part of the story is not mine to tell.' Whose is it? I'm ready for that part."

"Are you?"

"Peter, I've been patient."

"Aye, but that's not the same as being ready.

"Who's to say when that will be? You know, I was doing fine in southern California, just fine, and then my father, with whom I haven't communicated in nearly twenty years, sends me four negatives. It's as if he's decided, now that he's dead, to take an interest in me. As if he's directing me from the grave—and frankly, Peter, I'm feeling manipulated by both of you."

"Sorry. Not my intention."

"Then let's get on with it."

Peter sat quietly a few moments, looking toward the History Book Club, which seemed too raucous to be discussing a Baptist from Missouri. Then he said, "There is more for you to learn, John. But to learn some things, not just hear them, you have to be ready. One day when I was a wee lad in Scotland, my father was loading barrels onto a truck. I wanted to be a real man, you know.

"'Dad, let me help load the barrels.'

"'No,' he says, 'not till you're older.'

"I keep pestering him, and he must be growing mighty weary of it, so finally he says, 'All right, then.' He passes me one, and it falls right to the ground. A miracle it didn't smash my toes. Then he says, 'Lad, learn a lesson, will you? You have to be ready to carry some loads.'"

"That's condescending, Peter. I'm no laddie, and you're not my father."

"Fair enough."

"Will you tell me the rest of the story?"

"No, only you can complete the story. But I'll do my part in finishing this chapter. Please, give me just two more days."

"And what will I get out of it?"

"Two more stories."

"They better be good ones."

"Let's meet tomorrow, right after lunch. It'll involve a little hiking. You'll probably need a sweater."

The next day, John walked directly from the Bay View Café to The Pelican. Peter was waiting next to his pickup, wearing baggy shorts and hiking boots. A new cigar, still in cellophane, was sitting in his shirt pocket.

Peter said, "I've got drinks if we get thirsty. All set?"

"Let's go."

Burns was in his co-pilot's seat, panting with eagerness.

They drove a short distance past the bridge and turned right onto a strip of dirt that had room for a few parked cars.

Peter held up his cigar. "You mind?"

"Go ahead."

Peter found a trail that followed an old fence for about a hundred yards before it cut across an open field sloping down toward the bluffs. A large sign was posted near the start of the trail: "BEWARE! Mountain Lions." A paragraph of smaller print followed, indicating that cougars had been seen in the area and giving instructions on what to do if you encounter one, which John read but wanted to study, being both a lawyer inclined to fine print and a hiker inclined to fear, but Peter wouldn't slow his pace.

Peter hollered over his shoulder, "Not to worry, lad! I've never even seen paw prints." Then he chuckled and said, as if to himself, "Not that I have any idea what paw prints looks like."

Burns led the way, covering at least three times the distance, running ahead and running back, exploring ravines and sniffing God knows what. Peter was about twenty feet in front of John, puffing like an old locomotive. They descended to a trail that ran along the edge of the bluffs. The view was panoramic—north and south along the coastline, and west toward a horizon that faded from deep blue into a pale haze. Overhead, gulls, cormorants, terns, and oystercatchers beat against the wind and rested on currents, and below, waves broke gently against rocks.

"Grand day!" Peter exclaimed.

They turned south, following a serpentine trail around peninsulas and into coves. It led to a bench of weathered wood. Affixed to the backrest was a little metal plaque: "In memory of Ernest Balyeat, 1901–1998."

"Here we are," said Peter. "Your father and I came here a lot. In all weather. Sometimes we'd get soaked by crashing waves."

His cigar had gone out, and he held what remained in his right hand. They sat a few minutes, silent, enjoying the view.

"The first story," Peter said.

John mimicked a drum roll.

"It's about St. Francis of Assisi, who happened to be in the town of Gubbio when the residents were terrorized by a fierce wolf. The animal devoured other animals and attacked any human who happened to be alone. The people were so afraid they almost never ventured beyond the town walls unless in a well-armed group.

"Francis had compassion on the townsfolk, so he resolved to go out and meet the wolf. Everyone tried to prevent him. He was sure to be eaten. But Francis didn't become a saint without reason, did he? He commended himself to the protection of God and went out the town's gate.

"A multitude went with him but soon drew back. His fellow brothers followed him farther, but they, too, were afraid to get close to where the ravenous animal was known to prowl. So Francis walked on alone.

"Suddenly, the wolf came charging out of the woods directly toward Francis, its jaws wide open. But Francis stood his ground as the wolf approached, and then, when the beast was almost upon him, calmly lifted his hand and made the sign of the cross. And at the sign of the cross the wolf stopped. It walked slowly toward Francis and lay at his feet.

"'Brother Wolf,' he said, 'in the name of Christ I command you neither to harm me nor anyone else. You've killed God's creatures, both animals and those made in his image. You deserve death. But I offer you peace. The people will forgive your offenses, and because hunger has driven you to terrible acts, they will feed you and make sure you don't starve. For your part, you must never hurt or kill anyone again.' The wolf bowed his head and wagged his tail to signal his agreement with the terms of this compact.

"'Brother Wolf, in the name of Christ I command you to follow me so we can ratify this peace.' The wolf, meek as a lamb, followed Francis back to the town where a great multitude had gathered in wonder. Francis commended the wolf to the town's safekeeping, and with one voice the people promised to feed him till the end of his days. Then Francis asked the wolf to promise never to harm anyone again, and the animal, to show his consent, lifted a paw and placed it on the hand of Francis.

"For the next two years, the wolf lived peaceably in the town, going from door to door, where the people received him courteously and fed him well. He died of old age, a beloved part of the community."

Peter stopped speaking. The only sounds were from the waves.

John said, "That's it?"

"Aye."

"You want to know what I think it means?"

"Not till you've thought about it."

Thirty-One

The meaning seemed obvious: his father had confronted the wolf and made peace with it. Why didn't Peter just say that? Why the indirection? John's impatience warmed into anger every step back to the pickup. The stench of Peter's cigar, the Great Sage act, and the assumption that John would passively play along and then show up at The Pelican that evening—it all irked him. No wonder his congregation had fired him.

Peter parked in front of The Pelican and said, "See you this evening?"

"Will it be worth my time to stay? No offense, but I'm not sure today was worth it. Logan Stanhope made peace with . . . what? The death that haunted him? His guilt? Well, good for him. Too bad he couldn't have made peace with his wife and son."

"Aye, too bad. But who said the story was about your father? Everyone has wolves lurking in the shadows. A lot depends on what we do with them. Or what they do to us."

"For a defrocked minister, you're damn preachy."

"You sound like your father."

"And others, I would guess. But about tomorrow—I assume your big mystery has to do with the woman in the picture, right? Will you finally introduce us?"

Peter nodded. "Meet me here tomorrow at eleven."

John skipped The Pelican that evening, in no mood for banter and a broken piano. He had dinner at Little River Inn and called Megan with a report on what had happened that day.

The next morning Peter was waiting on the steps of The Pelican. "So—you ready?"

"As far as I know." John started to get into the pickup.

"We're walking this time." Peter pointed west down Main Street.

Burns seemed to know their destination. He was no longer a sheep dog but a sled dog, trotting three steps in front of them with his head erect. Peter greeted passersby, pausing to bestow a few hugs.

They walked to the end of Main, turned right for a dozen yards and then left again, down a dirt road to a two-story house. Its redwood siding had surrendered in the war against weather. Boxes of geraniums, deflowered by wind, sat beneath each window, including two dormers on the second floor. Around a vague lawn stood pickets that swayed like soldiers after a hard night of partying.

Burns leaped over the gate, bounded up the porch, and pushed open the door with his nose. His wagging tail disappeared inside before they reached the steps.

John told himself to relax. She was the one who should be nervous.

"Darlin', we're here," Peter said as he led them into the living room.

There she was: looking out the window toward the ocean. Her nose, distinctive cheekbones, and full lips were still beautiful, perhaps more so with the softening of years, and her hair, thick and long, was now streaked with white, giving the impression of water streaming down black rock. She did not turn toward John, which seemed more regal than rude.

Not until her right hand moved did John become aware that she was sitting in a motorized wheelchair. With difficulty she wrapped three fingers around a small knob and pushed it to turn the chair toward them.

The woman who had haunted his life was now before him. It was the same beautiful face, half hidden in shadow. Except light from the window fell directly on her face and revealed that its right side, from underneath her eyes to below her jaw, was not shadow but a birthmark of catastrophic ugliness.

"At last," she said, "we finally meet. My name is Lucia."

Thirty-Two

John's memory of the next few minutes would always be blurred. He would see only indistinct forms and movements in Lucia Morales's living room; he would hear fragments of sentences, none of which came from his own tongue-tied mouth. Peter, he thought, made formal introductions and kissed Lucia on the cheek—the ugly side, he was sure of that—and then left them alone. Burns stayed, keeping his head on Lucia's leg. She must have invited John to sit down, for as the day came into sharper focus, he would be in an overstuffed chair a few feet from her and she would be slightly to his right.

"Cup of coffee?" she asked. "I made a fresh pot, and if you don't mind helping yourself, it's in the kitchen."

"No, thanks. I've had plenty."

"You could probably use something stronger right now."

"Maybe, to be honest."

"I trust we'll both be."

John didn't know what to say. Nothing seemed appropriate.

She said, "With your permission, I'll begin."

He nodded. "Please."

She said, "Burnsie, excuse me." She rolled her chair to a large bookcase and pointed, with a deformed finger, in the general direction of a drawer near the bottom. "Would you please open that for me? And that large envelope on top? Would you put it on my lap?"

After they returned to their original places, she managed to draw from the envelope a print of *Nude on the Beach*. She raised it as close to her face as her arm allowed. "Much different? My hair is getting white. Parts of me not so firm, though that's more information than you need." She laughed and shook her head. "Do you see, John, how accurately this portrays me? That's the heart of this story. But I'm getting ahead of myself.

"About a year before this was taken, I had come up from a little village near Zacatecas. The journey through Mexico was hard. Things happened that I've spent years trying to forget. My father had died, and my mother and I had no means of support. I could have gone to Mexico City, I suppose, and become a prostitute. But with this face? A better option, it seemed, was to get to Tijuana, where my cousin was assisting people across the border. It was scary—the middle of the night, the cement drainage ditch, the flood-lights from helicopters. But we made it, most of us. My cousin had a contact in Chula Vista, who had a contact in L.A.—that's how it goes—and within a few weeks, I ended up in Monterey working two jobs. Days, I changed linens for a hotel in Pacific Grove, and evenings, I washed dishes at a restaurant in Monterey. That's where I met your father.

"One evening two servers got sick and had to leave, and the owner, desperate, sent me out to wait tables. (Imagine how desperate he had to be to send *me* out there!) My English was pretty good, but I was so nervous I could barely hold the dishes. Your father, at a table with two friends, smiled and whispered, 'You're doing fine.' Just a simple thing, really, but . . . he was a kind man.

"I must have done fairly well, because the owner sent me out the next evening, too, and the one after that, and before long I was a regular waitress. About a week later your father came back, this time by himself. We talked a few minutes, that's all. I didn't see him again for about two months, not until we ran into each other at Safeway. That's where we had our first real conversation, in the produce department, in front of bananas. He asked me questions, such as where I was from and did I have a family and how long had I been in the country. That set me on edge, being illegal. He told me about his work, his photography, and you visiting him for the summer. And then, before we went our separate ways, he gave me his card and said, 'Most of my work is with landscapes. But I've been thinking of doing something with models in natural settings. I'll pay well. Nothing sleazy, I assure you. You don't know me, but here—' He took back his card and wrote two names on the back, Ansel Adams and Wynn Bullock, and next to each he put a telephone number. 'Ever heard of these guys? No? They're famous photographers. Ask about them in any of the galleries in Carmel. They'll vouch for me.'

"John, I was stunned. Before I could say anything, my hand instinctively shot up to my face as if to protect it.

"Logan said, 'I will not embarrass you. You will have the final say on any print. We will destroy anything you don't like.'

"His words, though, weren't what convinced me. There was just something about him that allowed me trust him.

"So on my next day off, the only one I'd have for a while, we met at Point Lobos. I was afraid, having never done anything like this before. So was he, he later admitted. But he was a gentleman, a professional in every way.

"Two weeks later we met in the gallery where he did part-time work. You know the one, on Ocean Avenue. We were in the back room, next to a large work table. He laid a print on it and said, 'This is the only one I like. What do you think?'"

Lucia looked at the photograph in her lap, not saying anything for a moment. When finally she spoke, her words were soft and slow.

"Try to imagine growing up with a face like mine. The taunting of children, the terror of mirrors. You know, in many ways, you are your face. You can lose an arm, and that would disable you but not necessarily destroy you. But your face? How can you separate your face from your self? So much of who you are gets expressed through your face. Half of me was beautiful, but the other half? A nightmare. Who was I? The confusion, the shame, the self-loathing—it was awful.

"I don't mean to sound self-pitying. I just want you to understand what happened when I saw Logan's photograph. There I was: the whole me, the attractive and the ugly. Yes, my face appears hidden in shadow. That's what you and the world saw. In fact, I had come out of the shadow. Your father and the camera didn't lie." Lucia paused, looked down at *Nude on the Beach* again, and said, "And it was beautiful. *I* was beautiful. It would be an exaggeration to say Logan's art healed me. But this much is surely true: it began the healing."

The woman in a wheelchair had spoken with deep feeling. Her story had moved John. It did not, though, sweep away two decades of bitterness.

He said, "I'm happy for you, Lucia. But that picture ended up killing a person and maiming another."

She said, "I believe it's time for you to talk."

Thirty-Three

"Sorry for my harshness. Things were difficult for us."

Burns was curled next to Lucia's wheelchair, asleep. Sunlight had moved across the floor and illuminated his right ear, turning it into a lazy flame on his head.

Because Lucia had begun with *Nude on the Beach*, it seemed appropriate to do the same. Her eyes had the gravitational pull of black holes, sucking words out of him. He recounted seeing her on the beach and hearing his father's voice, although he didn't mention his discovery of what you can do to yourself in a state of arousal; he tried to convey the devastation they felt when his father left, and how the poster, when it became famous and was plastered everywhere, was like mockery from his lover.

"Are you implying that he left your mother for me?"

"It wasn't hard to figure out, you know. It finally pushed Mom over the precipice."

"John, your father did not leave your mother for me. That is the truth."

He might have heard what Lucia said; he probably could have repeated it verbatim to prove he'd been listening. But long-held perspectives, formed in anger and grief, don't change easily. Sometimes you hear and feel an earthquake before it registers in your consciousness.

"You ended up with Dad, and I ended up with a broken woman who could barely string together two days of normalcy. You may not have known what was happening, but Dad, at least, should have guessed. If he gave us much thought."

"I can't say what he thought at the time. Please listen to me: we were not together. I did not see him again for over two years. After he showed me the print he moved to Mendocino and I continued working at the restaurant in Monterey."

"Why didn't you go with him?"

"Why would I? Our relationship was professional, and then it ended. We were not lovers. He did not leave your mother for me. Can I say it any clearer? I doubt your father even remembered me until the picture became popular. Then he started worrying. Would it push me into a public spotlight? Would that embarrass me, given my face? And—this was his biggest concern—what would it do to my undocumented status? These questions ate at him until one day he drove down to Monterey to find me. The owner of the restaurant, who had fired me to avoid trouble, wouldn't talk. No one would. Only after he finally convinced someone he wasn't an immigration officer, that he was concerned about my welfare, did he get a lead on my whereabouts.

"He found me sharing a room over a garage with three other women. He asked how I was doing and what my plans were, and at some point in the conversation—I don't know if he planned it—he encouraged me to come up here. He had friends, he said, and could help me find work and a place to stay. I was hesitant, of course. Afraid. But what options did I have? So I agreed, and a week later he and Peter came down in a little U-Haul van, as if I actually had furniture to move. At a thrift store we bought an old chair for me to sit on in the back of the van, so as not to risk getting pulled over for having three in the front seat.

"That's how my friendship with Logan and Peter began. Logan, especially, felt responsible for me. As he saw it, he had ruined my life. For a while, I was their *project*, and I resented it. But that didn't last long. Peter hired me to work in his kitchen and Logan found me a position as caregiver to an eighty-four-year-old woman, who, not incidentally, provided me a room right here. She had been a professor at Stanford. An extraordinary person. For six years I assisted her and learned from her and grew to love her. When she died, she left me this house."

"You and Dad were never—"

"I'm getting there. For years Peter and Logan were like my brothers. I was safe with them. I even understood their humor, which is embarrassing to admit. They had a funny way of teasing each other. I laughed at everything they said or did. And they treated me like a queen. We became inseparable.

"There was never any romance between me and either of them. Oh, there might have been the occasional flirtation or sexual innuendo. But only as a joke. Really, I think we were afraid to upset the status quo. If either of them had a date, we would cheer him on and insist on a full report, complete with details. I never dated, for obvious reasons.

"Six years ago I started dropping things, including an armful of dishes at The Pelican. And I would occasionally lose my balance. Peter and Logan noticed these things. Always my protectors. They insisted I see a doctor. But how? I was still undocumented. No insurance. One night, after a header off the porch, they took me to the emergency room and Peter assured the woman at the desk, a regular at The Pelican, that he was good for the bill. They did tests and urged me to see a neurologist. Yeah, right. How could we afford that?

"That's what led to The High Council Resolution, The Momentous Decision, The Mucho Mega Coin Flip—we called it a variety of things. Anyway, there we were, in the kitchen, wondering how we could find money for a specialist. Peter suggested that either he or Logan should marry me. I could become legal, and then, as a spouse, get on a health policy. It wouldn't have to change anything, Peter argued. Nothing more than a formality, a paper marriage.

"We each had another beer, which no doubt contributed to the impression it was a good idea. But who would do the honors? Neither Peter nor Logan wanted to seem unwilling, so they argued for the privilege. The only way to settle it, they decided, was to duel with pistols. I pointed out that we didn't have pistols, and in any event it might be better just to flip a coin rather than one of them getting killed. So Peter rummaged around in that purse-thingy he wears and found a quarter. As he flipped, your father called heads. Peter fumbled the catch and the coin bounced across the table onto the floor. Both of them dropped to their knees to see how it landed. Peter rolled over on his back as though dead and Logan looked up and said, 'Lucia, will you marry me?'

"Three days later, thanks to the mail-order ordination Peter bought after the Presbyterians booted him, I became Mrs. Logan Stanhope, your stepmother. Then I was legalized and duly enrolled in Logan's health insurance. All according to plan. Except—I was diagnosed with multiple sclerosis."

"So you married Dad but weren't really, you know, husband and wife?"

"Not at first. We weren't living together, weren't even pretending to be married. We reversed things, I guess. Most people fall in love and get married; we got married and fell in love. Our commitment seemed to create a space for love to grow.

"One night Peter and Logan came for dinner. About halfway through the meal, Peter got a call from The Pelican. A broken pipe or something. So he left, and Logan and I finished eating and washing dishes, and then we sat on the couch. He kept asking about my MS, kept prying into my feelings. And something broke inside me. All my fear of what might happen came gushing out. Logan held me while I wept and wept.

"'You're not alone,' he said. 'I'm with you all the way.' Not *we're* with you but *I'm* with you. That may not sound like much of a difference, but the shift was momentous. It surprised us both, I think. He didn't edit it, didn't bring Peter back into the conversation. For the next hour or so we sat in silence, holding hands, as what he had said reverberated between us—and that, strange to say, was our real marriage. No witnesses except God. No minister saying, 'You may now kiss the bride.' Although that's what he did. For the first time. Then a second time, and a third. One thing led to another, until we walked toward the bedroom. At the door he said, 'Do they do this in Mexico?' He picked me up and carried me across the threshold."

"What about Peter?"

"The next few months were difficult. But he loved us both, so eventually—sooner than I would have—he managed to be happy for us."

Burns jumped up, as if he knew we were talking about his master. He went to the front door and whimpered.

Lucia said, "He needs to go out."

"Actually, I wouldn't mind stretching my legs. I'll walk with him."

"Good idea. Take your time. I've gotten used to an afternoon snooze."

Thirty-Four

The wind had freshened, and the grass on the headlands waved chaotically. John wished he had a heavier coat. They crossed the street and walked down a trail that led to another one along the bluffs. Burns turned right and John followed. They were soon blocked by a family of tourists—a man photographing his wife and children and two corgis, a risky enterprise so close to the edge. Burns sniffed one of the corgis, but she was Queen Elizabeth with a commoner.

Burns remained three steps ahead, leading them around the familiar loop. John, to steady nerves and to give Lucia more time, stopped at Patterson's Pub. Burns refused to enter, clearly embarrassed to be there. But the Pelican would have had distractions, Peter among them, and John needed solitude to nurse his righteous anger while it still had a pulse.

When they returned Lucia was where they had left her, wide awake. "Care for tea?" she asked. "No? Would you please pour me some? It'll make you nervous to watch, but I can still hold a cup. Usually."

John got the tea, situated himself on the couch, and said, "May I ask a question?"

"Anything."

"If Dad didn't leave Mom because of you, why did he?"

"Parts of your father were shut off. Dead-bolted. Only rarely would they be opened enough for a glimpse inside. I didn't like that about him. But people get to be who they are, don't you agree?"

Afternoon light deepened the darkness of her birthmark. It would have been almost frightening except for the softness of her eyes and the contrasting beauty of the other side.

"About a year ago your father said something that was a clue. We were watching a segment on the news about the effects of trauma, and when it was over he said quietly, 'Too bad I didn't get counseling.' I asked what he meant, but the door shut again, quickly."

"The wounds of war? Peter's theory?"

"I suppose. To you, he seemed so strong—your brave Daddy and all." She studied the cup in her hand. "But to himself, he felt like this cup, cracked. And there he was, the husband of a woman who was also cracked. I'm surmising in some of this, but as I said, parts of him occasionally opened a little, and when they did, I tried to see into the shadows. He believed he couldn't share his feelings with her. Maybe he was right, maybe wrong, I don't know. He imagined being added to the prayer concerns of her church. She would have turned it into a matter of faith, or to be more precise, his lack of faith. And what if he didn't get better? What if healing didn't come? She would possibly become worse, along with him. And what would happen to you?"

"Did he think divorce would help?"

"Divorce? He didn't consider it, not at first. He simply wanted— thought he needed—more time away, more time for an art he hoped might glue together what was coming apart inside him."

"Maybe that's what he told you, but I was there when Mom received the letter saying he wasn't coming home, that we were on our own."

"Did you see it?"

"Yes, she was holding it in her hand when I walked into the room."

"But I mean, did you read it?"

John had not actually read it. The implication of this crashed over him like a twenty-foot wave hitting a sandcastle: he had assumed the accuracy of his mother's interpretation, had trusted the reaction of someone who, to put it mildly, did not have a consistent hold on reality. Did she read it accurately? Or did she read it with lenses that refracted the sentences through fear and jealousy?

"No," he finally said.

"He tried to make contact. Letters and calls. Should he have been more persistent? The question haunted him. But what if he forced his way back and made things worse for everyone? Maybe her version of reality provided some sort of stability. Was it right to disrupt that? Not knowing, he stayed away, and the longer he stayed away—"

"But why didn't he reconnect after Mom's death, after I was older?"

"He planned to, someday. But it got harder with each passing year. The way he saw it, you rose above the mess he left you and became a success. He was afraid of ripping off the scab. Maybe he was just afraid, simple cowardice. But I believe he intended to tell you. When we knew what was happening—the cancer—I encouraged him to invite you up here. No way. He couldn't imagine a deathbed scene and the vice it would put you in— hearing all this and at the same time seeing him dying. He didn't think it would be fair."

They heard footsteps on the porch. Lucia said, "That'll be Peter. He looks in on me about now."

Peter rapped on the front door and walked in. "Still blathering, I see. Sorry to interrupt."

She said, "Good timing, actually. John is probably ready for a break. I certainly am." She turned to John, "Peter and I need to be excused. Not only is he my best friend, he's my nurse. If I ever get within shouting distance of the Pearly Gates, I'm going to say I know Saint Peter. Not that that'll be enough to get me in."

Peter said, "Darlin', if you don't get in, none of us stand a chance. But without you, it wouldn't be heaven anyway."

She said, "John, I have a girl who fixes dinner some evenings. A young artist who needs the money. She'll be here in a few minutes. You'll stay won't you?"

The afternoon's conversation had left John depleted, almost disoriented, and he knew he had had enough conversation for one day. "Thank you, Lucia, but I probably need to be alone."

John walked down Main, accompanied by Burns, who cheerfully ignored his command to stay at The Pelican. They returned to Patterson's Pub, where Burns resumed his spot under the bench by the front door, and John went inside, found a small table in the corner, and ordered a burger and ale.

The server's nametag said "Solstice." John wondered how many joints her parents smoked to come up with the name.

When he finished, she cleared his plate and asked, "Another Red Seal?"

"No, thanks."

"OK, then, here's your check. Have a nice evening."

Thirty-Five

John expected to see Burns waiting for him. But apparently there had been too many people sitting on the bench; too much fondling of ears and teasing.

"Does your master know you're here, boy?"

"Wait'll Peter finds out where you've been."

The sun was easing toward repose, a full moon was rising, and the wind had stilled. Perfect evening for a walk. John turned down Little Lake toward the headlands. Without intending it, his pace quickened. He wanted to walk faster, to run, to run faster from . . . from what? He could answer only the impulse, not the question. He tossed his fleece behind a tree and found the gait of legs and lungs that had been his way of coping with confusion.

The sunset in front of him had cast a barely discernible shadow on the ground behind him. He noticed it when he looked back to see if cars were approaching, and he checked it a moment later, and again after that. The shadow grew more distinct as he ran; it followed hard, chased him, threatened him. It was a ghostly embodiment of the fear he was fleeing. The faster he ran, the faster it followed. It wouldn't stop. Of course it wouldn't stop: it was created by him, part of who he was. And it wasn't outside him but inside him. It had been invisible through simple ignorance or deflected anger or cowardly self-protection, but now, here it was, coming after him and he could not outrun it: he had misjudged his father. His misjudgment had intensified his condemnation and his condemnation had confirmed his misjudgment. And worse, there *was* worse: he had passed all this on to his mother, directly or indirectly, and he had set her up for the torture of the poster. He had promoted a lie that had pushed her over the edge of sanity.

In the coming months and years John would fit everything into a larger picture; he would take into account that he was a teenager at the time, that both his father and mother had mental problems, and that everyone, after all, makes mistakes and some make death-dealing mistakes. But not that evening, not when the shock of awareness had collapsed time and dangled before him his mother's blue face and limp body.

He swatted at the image, as if beating away bats in the dark. An oncoming car slowed and passed him with a wide curve, keeping away from the crazy man with flailing arms. The weight of his new knowledge caused him to stumble. He could run no farther. He bent over and heaved up the burger and bile.

Another car approached. This one stopped, and the driver rolled down the window and asked, "Need help?"

"No, thanks. I'm fine." He just realized he killed his mother, but other than that, he was fine. Another car approached, and he jumped off the road and wandered through the tall grass toward the bluff. He could hear waves, knew the edge had to be close. He sat down, or maybe the heaviness pushed him down. When tears came, he fell on his side and curled like the baby he once was in her womb.

He must have fallen asleep at some point, for suddenly the moon was brighter and the night darker, and he was shaking violently in the cold. He sat up. The surf seemed deceptively benign in the moonlight. Would there be enough light to walk back?

In the left corner of his vision, something moved. But nothing was there. He must have imagined it. Then a few seconds later he was certain of an indistinct, shadowy presence. He squinted. The brain can be slow to process information it doesn't want to receive. A dog, he thought. A dog with a very long tail. No, it must be a cat. A very large cat.

Thirty feet away stood a mountain lion.

Terror bolted through him. His entire reality became one indivisible and inescapable fact: an animal at the top of the food chain had found its dinner.

He couldn't move. Not one muscle would cooperate. Had he managed to get up, he would have run for all he was worth and a second later he wouldn't have been worth much because the lion would have ripped open his jugular vein.

He stared at the lion. The creature stared back, motionless. Later, when able to think it, John wished he had calmly told the lion that it was loved by the Creator, and that miraculously the lion had held out its paw. But John was no saint. What he really said was "Don't even fucking think of taking one more step toward me."

The lion must not have heard him.

Slowly, a front paw moved in John's direction, and then a hind leg. The upper lip lifted to bare teeth. John's life was coming to an end. Adrenaline unfroze his body and he jumped to his feet. As the lion started to lunge, Burns exploded out of the grass to divert its attention, to offer himself, the good shepherd for his sheep. By the time John realized what had happened the lion was running through the grass with Burns's neck in its jaws.

Did John find part of Burns's body in the grass? If so, what did he do with it? The first thing he clearly remembered was Peter saying, "My God, lad, what happened? You look like you've been in a war." Blood was smeared on his hands and shirt.

Peter guided John to his table and told Patch to get a wet towel and brandy and to be quick about it. Peter wiped him off, as best he could, and said, "Now, take your time. Have a wee drink." His voice was warm as the brandy.

John's halting story rambled incoherently. Patterson's . . . running . . . mother—avoiding the inevitable. The bluff . . . the lion . . . the terror—he delayed as long as possible, until at last he had to say, "Peter, Burns saved my life." Instantly, Peter knew. He dropped his forehead on the table and let out a terrible wail. No one spoke; no one moved. John raised a blood-stained hand toward Peter's shoulder but thought better of it. He had no idea what to do, yet he sensed everyone wanted him to do something, to relieve whatever pain he had inflicted.

All he could do was weep, which didn't seem to help much. So he got up and went behind the bar and took a nearly-full bottle of bourbon. On the way back to the Alegria he made significant progress toward finishing it before passing out on his bed.

Thirty-Six

The pounding. Where was it? It moved from his dream to his head to his door.

"John, you OK?" Peter hollered. "Past noon, lad."

John groaned, loudly enough for Peter to hear him.

"Well then, you're alive. Can you be at Lucia's in an hour?"

John groaned again, which Peter misinterpreted as assent.

"Good. See you then."

It took longer than an hour to haul himself out of bed and into the shower, drink two cups of coffee, and buy aspirin. But arriving twenty minutes late wasn't bad, all things considered. Peter opened the door and motioned for him to sit on the couch. Lucia was in her usual place by the window.

Peter said, "I told her what I know."

She shook her head in sympathy.

Peter said, "A reporter from the *Beacon* called this morning. It's not every day someone encounters a lion around here. And Burns. Everyone knew him. So—"

"I'm sorry, Peter. I . . . I . . ." A lump knotted inside John's throat.

Peter held up his hand to stop John from speaking. "You aren't responsible for Burns's death. He was a good dog, doing his duty. Losing him, though, so soon after your father—it's an overwhelming grief, that it is." He found a tightly balled handkerchief and pulled apart a few encrusted inches to service his nose. "Too much damn death. Everywhere you turn." He expelled a sigh that originated just outside the gates of Eden.

"I didn't know he followed me, I swear. I went for a walk and started running, and then it was as if I ran into something that flattened me."

"And what would that be?" Peter asked.

"Myself, I guess."

"Aye."

"After what you told me, Lucia, I realized I had made false assumptions, blaming you and especially my father for my mother's death. But I wasn't innocent, and the guilt—"

"You'll have to make peace with—"

"My wolf?"

Peter nodded.

Lucia said, "Peter, I need a shove. Would you straighten me before taking John upstairs?"

The top of the stairway opened into a large room. Along one wall was a small bed, and along the opposite, a wooden desk. In the center stood a table, maybe ten or twelve feet square, and on it were prints of varying sizes stacked in neat piles. Underneath the table were half-a-dozen cardboard boxes filled with negatives. On the walls, covering every inch from ceiling to floor, were prints of the same scene: a log-strewn beach and the sea beyond and the sky above. The camera's angle of vision hadn't changed even slightly, but each black-and-white photograph was unique. The clouds were merrymaking white or menacing black; the waves were tumult gone wild or tranquility at ease; the trees were bent by wind or brushed with sunset.

Peter said, "The darkroom is in the backyard, a wee building with no windows." He pointed to the desk. "He left you something over there. Take your time. I'm headed back to The Pelican."

On the left side of the desk were assorted cameras, large and small. On the right were rows of lenses, short and tall. In the center, near the wall, were pipes in a rack and a humidor, and on a well-worn ink blotter lay a handwritten letter. Three rolls of film served as a paperweight.

> Dear John,
>
> They say a picture is worth a thousand words. But I hope these words will be worth more than a thousand pictures.
>
> Please forgive me. I'm sorry I wasn't a better husband for your mother, or a better father for you. You both deserved better. I deeply regret everything I have done to hurt you. I have no right to expect, but I do hope for, your forgiveness.
>
> I love you. Now that the end has come for me, I have nothing else to say. So I'll say it again, I love you. I always have. And if

your mother's religion is true, I always will. (I'll find out before
too long).
Dad

P.S. Everything in this room is yours. Lucia agrees. Keep it,
sell it, or throw it away.

John sat motionless, paralyzed by feelings too sharp to ignore and too
complex to understand. After what might have been a long while, he picked
up the Hasselblad and buried his nose in its leather strap, breathing deeply
and detecting, he thought, sweat and tobacco.

When he went downstairs, Lucia asked him to stay a little longer, and
to stay upstairs. He accepted without hesitation, grateful for the invitation.
So while she napped, he returned to the Alegria, changed into running
clothes, and checked out. He ran south along the highway, not yet ready to
revisit the bluffs.

Bernice called as he was parking in front of Lucia's house. She wondered how he was doing. He told her about his encounter with the lion,
but didn't bring up the one with himself. She sounded weary, tired of over-
seeing the office and making excuses for him, and she suggested that Mr.
Lambert had come near the end of compassion, and if he pounced, no dog
would come to the rescue this time. Her work, she said, might be similar
to a sheepdog, but don't count on her to get dragged through the bushes
for him. John expressed understanding and asked to be connected to Mr.
Lambert's office, not expecting to be able to talk with him, but Ruth Corrigan immediately got him on the line. John expressed appreciation for the
kindness and patience shown him, stressed his commitment to the firm,
and withdrew his name from consideration for managing partner. The
words came easily, with little thought and no struggle. A few weeks earlier
this would have been unimaginable. But things happen, as Bernice said,
and sometimes what happens is a change of perspective so profound that
to maintain balance you have to shift the direction your feet are pointing.

That evening John and Lucia had started on a bottle of mediocre
Zinfandel before Peter arrived with a bottle of Chateauneuf-du-Pape he
had been saving for celebration but decided to open for consolation. They
toasted the memory of Logan Stanhope and Burns the Brave, and made
appreciative noises as the wine slid across their tongues.

Peter said, "Well now. We've unfinished business, don't you think,
Lucia?"

She seemed to know what he meant and nodded.

"John," Peter continued, "your father's been dead going on three months. Haven't you wondered about his remains?"

Actually, John hadn't thought much about them; he must have assumed they'd been buried or scattered somewhere.

Before John could answer, Peter said, "He's in your room."

"Up there?" John asked, incredulously.

"Aye. Did you notice the humidor on the desk?"

"Yes."

"He's in there."

John had a large swallow of Chateauneuf-du-Pape. And then another.

"It's good you didn't try smoking him, huh?" Peter laughed so hard he started coughing. "Mercy! Anyway, it didn't seem right to have the funeral without you. So we waited, didn't we, Lucia? But now that you're here, it's time. Not that I feel much like praying yet, especially public praying, but there comes a time to hoist your socks and do what's got to be done. Right?"

John wasn't sure whether it was the wine or the conversation that started the room spinning. Unfortunately, he didn't remain conscious long enough to set down his wine glass, and thus he created what Peter would refer to as a memorable stain on Lucia's couch.

Thirty-Seven

Regaining consciousness, John found himself on the couch, covered with a blanket. From the kitchen came laughter and pans clanging and the aroma of frying onions. During dinner they decided to hold the funeral a week later at—where else?—Portuguese Cove.

Before bed that night John made two phone calls. Pat Kolwolski was ready to embark on her voyage but promised to coax her old car up to Mendocino before donating it to St. Vincent de Paul. Megan seemed supportive but distant, like a member of a jazz ensemble waiting her turn. When she cut loose it was quite a riff: she missed him, obviously more than he missed her, which was understandable given what he had been through, but the fact that she understood made her realize how much she loved—yes, she wasn't afraid to say it—loved him and thus would wait, however long it took, for him to get home, assuming he was still coming back to her.

After variations of this theme played out, he said simply, "I need you. Please come up for the funeral as soon as you can." She agreed to ask for family emergency leave even though they weren't technically a family. The next day she reported that she would be arriving at SFO at 1:35 p.m. on Friday, two days before the service.

As John waited for Megan, his need for order asserted itself; he wanted to regain control of his life. So as morning's soft light stroked the crest of waves and turned two-dimensional darkness into three-dimensional day, he took the Hasselblad and a tripod to the bluffs. At first, he couldn't stop glancing over his shoulder for creatures on the prowl, but he knew the real danger came from what he didn't see. With only a little searching he found the spot where his father had stood; three holes remained in the caked dirt, and into each he dropped a leg of the tripod. The light meter took some fiddling to figure out. It gave a series of readings—each with a potential shutter speed and aperture size. But which one to use?

Humans see with shallow depth of field. Cameras can get everything in focus. Of course you may not want to see everything.

A shudder went through him. The f-stop, that's what he said controlled it.

The higher the number, the more in focus. Get it?

Those last words were so distinct his father could have been standing next to him.

Get it, Johnny? Do you finally get it?

He turned the f-stop ring to the highest number, f-22, and slowed the shutter speed to 1/15 of a second. He paused, motionless, for two or three minutes. This was his father's place, what he did, day after day and year after year. His ashes would be scattered here, thrown to the wind and water and whatever was behind them. But now John had a picture to make.

Click.

As simple as that, for the camera anyway.

It then seemed necessary to move on, to find his own place. So John hiked around the headlands until he came to an inlet framed by a delicate arch through which white foam pushed with anarchical exuberance. There he returned: every subsequent day, same scene, different picture. In early afternoon, after lunch had settled, he would run hard and long, and after cleaning up, he and Lucia and would open a bottle of wine and talk—story after story, each opening another part of their lives. Eventually they would walk and roll to The Pelican to join Peter for dinner. Jeffrey was back, grumpy as ever, with Faulkner now his fulltime assistant. Patch and Melinda moved between tables, anticipating orders before regulars placed them. Wing worked the bar, hopping from one stool to the next, gesticulating wildly. Meadowlark was so happy to see Lucia she fell on her with a breath-threatening hug. Louise showed up one evening, and after sitting down said, "I hate getting old," to which Lucia replied, "Beats the alternative."

This caused a moment of silence until Louise leaned over and cupped Lucia's face in her hands and kissed her forehead and said, "Thank you, dear."

Two evenings in a row John resisted requests to play the piano, but by the third, he surrendered and repeated imitations of Jerry Lee Lewis and Jimmy Swaggart, to the delight of Lucia, after which he told Peter that this time he wasn't kidding—no ifs, ands, or buts about it—he was never, ever going near that instrument until a certain tightwad wallet coughed up the bills to get it tuned.

Each night John awakened for a session of self-accusation. What if he had read his father's letters? What if he had allowed him into his life? What if he hadn't fed anger with a lie? What if he hadn't further disabled the mind of his mother? What if she had had a deeper understanding of his father's vulnerabilities? What if, what if, what if . . . ? He thrashed about until slowly, like drops of calming tonic, fragments of Lucia's conversations seeped into his consciousness. Eventually he would relax in her acceptance and—dare he think it?—her adoption of him, and sleep would return.

On Friday he left Lucia's house before the sun had risen. When it did, billowy banks of fog were resting on vineyards and curling around hills. In Cloverdale, after another cup of coffee, he lowered the top of his car; the morning promised a welcome change from the damp chill. Anticipation accelerated with each mile, and it became difficult to keep a lawful foot on the gas pedal. Marin County, Golden Gate Bridge, Nineteenth Avenue—down he sped, in and out of traffic, up and down hills, until he reached SFO two hours earlier than necessary. He wandered around newsstands and ate a gigantic cinnamon roll, the sugar making him as jittery as a hummingbird on cocaine. Eventually he spotted a bouncing redhead among the disembarking passengers and maneuvered toward her; when she leaped straight up about a foot, he knew Megan had seen him. She launched herself into his arms with a force that almost knocked him down.

As they merged onto north Highway 101 Megan asked, "So how long will it take to get to Mendocino?"

"On Friday afternoon? Four or five hours, maybe more. But we're not going there, not tonight."

"Can't wait to jump me?"

"Right, and I don't want to expose us—"

"I thought that'd be exactly what you want."

"Let me finish, will you? I don't want to expose us to the curves of Highway 128 while my mind is so distracted by other curves. Besides, we need time alone."

"So where're we going?"

"You'll have to wait and see."

"It'd better be special. You owe me for my longsuffering patience."

"You won't be disappointed."

And she wasn't, not when they entered the lobby of The Fairmont. He had reserved a room with a view of the bay, which they thoroughly enjoyed after he slipped a tip into the hand of the porter for carrying luggage they could have managed, and after he hung out the Do Not Disturb sign, and after they fell into bed as quickly as they could strip off clothes and pull back blankets, and after they completed the reintroduction of their bodies.

An old joke amongst John's fraternity brothers was that they wanted to get to know this or that girl in the biblical sense. They said it in pious tones, as if with righteous motives, but of course they meant *know* in the sense that Abraham knew Sarah and along came Isaac. The ancients were on to something, John thought. More than flesh is penetrated in the act: two individuals meet one another, completely. That's what it feels like anyway, but is this accurate? That's what he wondered, not for the first time that afternoon because it was over before he had had time to think, but the second time, about an hour later. Yes, they experienced deep intimacy. But was it a climax of knowledge? Maybe humans do this in hope that one more union will finally dispel the darkness, that they will at last know and be known, that the love they seek will finally have been made.

When they pulled themselves out of bed to dress for dinner (reservations at The Carnelian Room), Megan said, "Thanks."

"For what?"

"For not folding my underwear and stacking it in a neat pile before getting down to business."

"It's your special day."

Thirty-Eight

Megan and Lucia dismissed John from their "get acquainted meeting," and when he returned an hour later, they weren't finished. They told him not to hurry back. Wandering aimlessly, he noticed Pat Kolwolski emerging from the Mendocino Hotel, where she had just checked in, and after tears and laughter and repeated hugs, John took her to The Pelican where she and Peter instantly fell into memories of Logan Stanhope—a conversation that eventually morphed into heated agreement about the hopelessness of the current president. When enough time had lapsed to risk returning to Lucia's house, John was admitted back, albeit reluctantly. Megan and Lucia were now a team, bound by a cord woven out of love for him, an honest delight in the other, and something beyond his ken, perhaps ancient and tribal.

Early Sunday afternoon, John, Megan, and Lucia went to The Pelican for what Peter called a warm-up wake. When they arrived, Pat and Peter were already at his table. Pat was dressed in a tasteful black dress, and it occurred to John that he hadn't remembered to tell her the service would be at a hard-to-reach beach. Peter, for his part, had forsaken the leather kilt for a woolen plaid, presumably the McLeod tartan; white socks covered his calves, and tucked into the top of one was a dagger sporting an ornate gold handle; his waist-length jacket, dark tweed, gave off an odor of mothballs.

John introduced Megan and said, "Looking spiffy, Peter."

Peter said, "I clean up fairly well for funerals." The "r" in the last word trailed on for effect, his accent more pronounced than usual.

Megan said, "I think he's kind of cute."

Peter said, "Logan, I mean, John—that was a slip, wasn't it?—where'd you find such a smart girl?"

As they rearranged furniture to accommodate Lucia's wheelchair, Peter asked Patch to get glasses and a couple of bottles of Chardonnay, which they drained as they shared stories about Logan. Father Stu and Louise joined the circle, soon followed by Meadowlark and Wing; Jeffrey and Faulkner couldn't resist abandoning their posts and wedging themselves into the group. The only person missing was Bernice. Not that she knew Logan Stanhope. But John regretted not sending her an airline ticket. The circle would never be unbroken, in this life, but the rough geometry around the table expressed the new wholeness he felt.

At two o'clock the bell from the steeple of the Presbyterian Church tolled for a full minute.

Peter said, "There's our signal. Time to go." He stood abruptly and hoisted a glass in silent tribute to what lay ahead. Everyone at the table rose, gathered coats and shawls, and prepared to follow him to the Cove.

When the bell stopped ringing, a new sound assailed the air: a wheezing grunt followed by a piercing squeal, as if a large animal had been snagged under the axle of a truck; it grew louder and slowly formed itself into "Amazing Grace."

Peter said, "That would be Thomas, our piper. He'll be leading us."

The cortege walked down the center of Main toward the headlands. Immediately behind the skirling confusion—a strange mixture of Scottish Folk and American Gospel—marched Peter, formally, almost martially, holding the humidor of ashes against his chest, flanked by John, Lucia, and Megan on his left, and Pat on his right. Immediately behind them came Faulkner and Jeffrey and The Pelican regulars, and behind them, in increasing disarray, an assemblage of townsfolk, many of whom John had not met.

At the end of Main they turned left on a path that funneled them into single file and led through brush toward the edge of the bluff. After about thirty yards the path narrowed and became impassable for Lucia's wheelchair. Peter strode on, as if oblivious to the problem. Before John could say, "Now what do we do?" Faulkner and five other men appeared from behind; they surrounded the chair and, barely breaking stride, lifted it and continued walking. Megan let out a whimper of concern. How would they get her down a trail—if you could call it that—that was uneven, extremely narrow, and very steep? Ahead, the piper and Peter had already disappeared down it.

At the start of the descent, the team set down the chair. Faulkner whispered something in Lucia's ear, and then, with gentleness worthy of the

Madonna, wrapped one arm around her shoulders and slid the other under her knees and lifted her out of the chair. He wobbled for a moment, balancing himself, took a deep breath, and moved slowly forward with a team member in front warning of obstacles on the ground and another behind holding a hand on his back. John couldn't watch, but couldn't *not* watch.

The muscles around Lucia's eyes tightened and her brow furrowed, but she made not the slightest groan.

Megan kept whispering, "Oh God, oh God."

Not paying attention to his own steps, John slipped and almost took the direct route to the beach, making him even more nervous about Faulkner's undertaking. Eventually, though, they all reached the sand and rocks and driftwood. Their funeral chapel. Instead of flowers and furniture polish, the fragrance of salt and seaweed; instead of an electric organ and quiet whispers, the sound of surf and gulls; instead of pall bearers ushering them to pews, Peter ushering them to a place scouted out earlier, where he turned his back to the water, dropped the humidor at his feet, and waited for them to get situated around him.

"Sit down everyone," he said. "Make yourself as comfortable as possible. John and Megan, you'll be over here, please." He pointed to a log near him where he expected them to sit. "And Pat, too. Aye, that's lovely. Thank you."

Faulkner lowered Lucia onto the sand next to them and propped her against the log. She grimaced and shook her head. Faulkner adjusted her angle, but that, too, failed to work. She motioned with her hand, and he seemed surprised but moved her onto her side, straightened her legs, and rolled her onto her stomach. Enough upper body strength remained, apparently, for her to rest on elbows, like a young woman sunning herself in a bikini.

Or without a bikini.

Lucia winked at John, and they both smiled.

Megan whispered, "What? What's so funny?"

Pat, holding a shawl tightly around her shoulders, reached over with her free hand and gripped John's leg. She leaned close and said, "Love you, buddy." A lump of emotion rose suddenly to the back of his throat.

Peter began. "Jesus said, 'I am the resurrection and the life,' and we certainly hope so, don't we? I can't imagine how any of us wouldn't hope to God he was right. Because here we are, remembering Logan Stanhope. It's a fitting place, this stretch of beach. No one has seen it more clearly than

Logan. Maybe he's seeing it now, for all we know. What I do know is that we're not alone. We have each other. And we have a grief that, to tell the truth, feels unbearable. I miss my friend. So do you, I'm sure. There'll be no sugarcoating our sadness, but it'd be selfish to let sadness keep us from giving thanks for his life."

A dog barked down the beach, the sound carried by an insistent wind; gulls kept up a cacophonous chorus; large waves slammed nearby rocks and broke close to the beach.

Peter then introduced Pat to the group and asked her to read Psalm 139, "except the last bit, the curses against the wicked that no one wants to hear." She did her best to be heard, speaking clearly, until her voice cracked with "If I take the wings of the morning and dwell in the uttermost parts of the sea, even there thy hand shall lead me." She paused a few seconds before continuing. "Even the darkness is not dark to thee, the night is bright as day; for darkness is as light with thee . . ."

She continued reading, but John's thoughts went no further. Is the darkness really light with God? The darkness that swallowed his mother? The darkness from which his father fled? The darkness that had been in him? Was the poet saying that God sees into the darkness? Or saying more, that God creates light from the darkness? As Pat made her way back to their log and Father Stu came forward for the New Testament reading, an affirmation from St. Paul that nothing, not even death, shall separate us from the love of God, John knew the questions would stay with him a long time.

Peter said something about sharing memories later at The Pelican but "wouldn't it be fitting to have his son, John, offer a few words at this time?"

John had not been warned, although he suspected something like this might happen. He stood and turned toward the group but the words were buried under a weight of loss that made it impossible to speak.

Peter put his arm around John's shoulder and guided him back to the log, and then he helped Louise stand and stood next to her for support as she read from the *Book of Common Prayer*.

"Give courage and faith to those who are bereaved, that they may have strength to meet the days ahead . . ." John glanced at Lucia. Her strength had given out, and she was now lying flat, resting half her face on the sand. A stream of tears glistened against the dark of her birthmark. ." . . Rest eternal grant to him, O Lord: and let light perpetual shine on him."

When Louise had finished, Peter lifted the humidor out of the sand and, cradling it in his left arm, said, "'O death, where is thy sting?' the apostle asks. Where is it? Right here, if you ask me! The sting of death is your best friend reduced to ashes. The sting of death is what Logan carried in him all his life, what is in all of us, what most of us do our sorry best to cover with drink or sex or money or power—to name a few of my favorites—but my friend here covered with beauty, aye *beauty*, with an art that used both black and white to make something memorable.

"And that's what he did with his life, didn't he? Made something memorable of it, something we'll never forget . . ." He stopped, unable to go further, and dropped his head for a few moments, searching for equilibrium to carry on. Not finding it, he shook his head in resignation and went over to Lucia, knelt down, and gently leaned his cheek against the dark purple of her face and released tears that ran off his face onto hers.

Megan said, "I can't watch this."

Peter turned Lucia over and lifted her and motioned for Faulkner to provide a backrest with his own body. Then Peter resumed his homily. "Aye, the sting of death. Feels like we got out of bed in the middle of the night and a scorpion got us good. But morning is coming, that's what I have to believe. We might still be limping, but the sun will rise and beat the hell out of the night. Maybe that's what faith is about, the faith I'm not good at, that I've spent most of my life questioning. Maybe it's not about certainties but about finding just enough hope to pull you into another day. If Scripture's to be believed—and today I want to—that's what the resurrection of Jesus must give us. Enough hope to go on. Otherwise . . ."

Peter did not finish the sentence. He turned and walked toward the surf, pausing at its edge. Then he waded in—shoes and all. Water washed over his knees and then his thighs. As the remains of Logan Stanhope's body were about to be scattered to the elements, John was thinking about Peter's body, and he realized that, if Peter didn't stop walking, they'd see revealed the mystery of what he wore under his kilt.

Black briefs, it turned out. He pulled his kilt up around his waist and kept walking until water covered his stomach. He took the lid off the humidor and held it high, waiting. They all saw it coming: a wave that grew in size and speed. Peter did not move; he held his ground, facing the wave, as if daring it to strike him.

When it did, it broke directly over him and threw him under. He was lost from sight and did not surface.

Megan said, "Where is he?"

John said, "I don't know."

Too much time was passing. Everyone, except Lucia, stood and was searching the water.

Meadowlark screamed, "There! On the right, see? Near the rocks."

Faulkner said, "A rip current must've got him."

When he crawled out of the water and stood, it was clear the wave had had its way with him. One shoe was gone, both socks had fallen around his ankles, and his kilt was still up around his waist. He held the humidor, though, and turned it upside down to let it drain. He smiled and pumped the humidor above his head.

"Aye!" he shouted. "Finished!"

Lucia started the laughing, and it continued, until after The Pelican closed and they were outside, under its sign, and the single bulb that lit the sign illuminated their faces, but only partially, leaving much to the night. They were all Lucia now, John noted, as in their inmost being they always had been and always would be. And it would be enough—the shadowy beauty, the failing love—it would be enough, if they held each other in the widening circle of grace.

Epilogue

The curator who hung *Nude on the Beach* on a freestanding wall in a room at the Norton Simon Museum was Megan. Megan Stanhope, now. We were married at All Saints Episcopal Church in Pasadena six months after my father's funeral. Peter grumped about not presiding at the ceremony, but his sketchy qualifications, among other things, earned Megan's veto. He stood next to the groom, however, as proudly as Megan's sister attended the bride. He also took charge of the bagpiper who led us and our guests out of the sanctuary and across the street to the hotel for the reception.

We cajoled Pat to delay her trip for a year to help sort through my father's negatives and make suitable prints for The Logan Stanhope Retrospective which, following the Norton Simon exhibit, toured the country for sixteen months. It found a grateful audience in a nation reeling from the horror of 9/11.

I resigned from Lambert and Wilson, and Megan and I moved to Mendocino, where we purchased a two-story building on Main Street, a few doors from The Pelican. The street-level entrance leads into the *Stanhope Gallery*, and the outside stairs lead up to the office of *John Stanhope, Attorney-at-Law*. Twice a week we have dinner with Lucia, whose health remains steady. We miss Peter. He flew to Honolulu to become first mate on *Tuesday's Child*. The last we heard from him came on a smudged postcard from Vanuatu. So in addition to assisting Megan with the gallery and establishing my practice, I oversee Jeffrey and the rest of the staff at The Pelican, doing my best to hold things together until Peter returns to take his necessary place in our community. It may seem greedy to hope that Pat will join him (and us) here, but it's a reasonable possibility, considering the inheritance already bestowed by Logan Stanhope.

Acknowledgments

I would like to thank the following people who read early drafts of this novel: Tansy Chapman, Stephne and Woody Garvin, Tom Leedy, Chip Macgregor, Joy McCullough-Carranza, Matilda McLaughlin, Susan and John Mitchell, Karen and Michael Moreland, Rachel Rose Nelson, Garry Schmidt, Debbie Turnbull, and Elaine Welty. Their comments undoubtedly strengthened my story, but because I didn't always heed their advice I alone bear responsibility for the remaining weaknesses.

My wife, Shari, is always my first reader. In this case, she was also the first listener. Before a single word was written, I thought it would be fun to tell her the story orally, as if we were in the living room with a bottle of wine. But we were in the car, driving north from San Diego. Two hundred miles later, beyond Santa Barbara, she interrupted to ask if she could visit a bathroom. Did I mention I was driving? I barely knew where we were, and it may count as a miracle that we weren't in an accident. Beyond listening to my blathering, Shari read every subsequent draft, as well as absorbed, in her gentle way, my frustrations and fears. She supplied the encouragement to keep me writing and, as in everything, the love that makes me continually grateful for our marriage.

I have tried to be factually accurate in my descriptions of Mendocino, California, with one exception: The Pelican Bar and Grill is entirely a product of my imagination. The same must be said about characters in the story. But *similarities* with actual people may not be entirely coincidental. (Isn't this the point of fiction?) If anyone is offended, call me and I'll buy lunch. And that goes for anyone upset about *not* being included. I suggest we meet at The Pelican.

This book took many years to complete, in part because of other endeavors. I began writing when we lived near San Diego, always imagining that my protagonist would end up in Mendocino. What I could not have imagined was this: about halfway through the first draft—*just as John Stanhope is driving into Mendocino*—I received a telephone call from John Turnbull, asking if I would interview for the position of pastor of Mendocino Presbyterian Church. I ended up serving that wonderful congregation and community for nearly seven years. Make of that what you will.

Finally, my parents. My mother, now in her nineties, continues to offer love and support. And my father, unlike the one in my story, upheld more than his share of a great father-son relationship. Among his other influences, he introduced me to books, photography, and the God he served so faithfully. I will always miss him. To his memory I gratefully dedicate this book.